LICENSE TO FLIRT

ELIZABETH GERTRUDE

Contents

1

CHAPTER 1

Santa Ana in August was hot and dry. The sun baked the streets, sidewalks, and anything else in its path. Sweat was inevitable, even in the refuge of shade or with the assistance of a fan. The city's citizens were either cooped up inside with their air conditioning on full blast, or at the beach in the cool water. I was one of the cooped up. Three fans directed toward me and my shirt still clung to my chest and back with perspiration. A tall red head skipped past my room sporting a pair of jean shorts and a bikini top.

"Vivian Tyler, where are you going?" I yelled after her, unwilling to get up from my seat in front of the rotating fans.

"I'm heading to the beach, Xavier and Erik are picking me up. Want to come?" She popped her head into the door frame of my room just in time to catch me shake my head in response. "I figured; see you in a couple hours!" The front door slammed behind Vivian and I sprang up, pulling off every item of clothing I had been wearing. Now fully naked, I was free to let the fans cool off every part of my body.

My fingers scrolled through a playlist on my phone and settled on "Baby Got Back" by Sir Mix-a-Lot. My silly choice of music couldn't and wouldn't be made fun of by my best friend now that she had left, so I wasted no time in letting lose. My hips moved to the beat of the song, matching each phrase, loop, and hook. I used a toothbrush as my microphone, rapping along with the voice that spilled through my speaker system.

"'Well, use me, use me'Cause you ain't that average groupieI've seen them dancin'To hell with romancin'She's sweat, wet,Got it goin' like a turbo 'VetteI'm tired of magazinesSayin' flat butts are the thing'"

I held out my toothbrush to my fake audience as I spat out the lyrics.

"'So, fellas! (Yeah!) Fellas! (Yeah!)Has your girlfriend got the butt? (Hell yeah!)Tell 'em to shake it! (Shake it!) Shake it! (Shake it!)Shake that healthy butt!Baby got back!'"

Suddenly the doorbell rang and my heart lurched from my chest. Quickly pulling on my robe, I tied it tightly around my body and scrambled toward the door. With the music playing quietly in the background, I opened the door and sucked in a fearful breath. The man in front of me towered over my small stature by at least a foot, making my body tremble with intimidation. But it wasn't just his tall and muscly physique that led to my trembling knees, it was his god damn gorgeousness. His dark brown hair was slicked to the side, mirrored aviator sunglasses shielded his eyes from me, and he wore a blue police uniform that clung to every contour of his body.

"Sorry to disturb you Miss." He smiled charmingly down at me and I forced a girlish giggle back down my throat.

"I-It's no problem, Officer. What can I do for you?" I bit my lip, moving some hair away from my face. His penetrating stare was hard to match, so I settle for looking at his name tag.

Officer Rivera

"I'm just going around the neighborhood introducing myself. I'm moving in next door to you." His voice echoed with a hint of a Spanish accent as he pointed to the old Jones's house that had been sitting for sale for almost a year.

"Oh, well, welcome to Ophelia Avenue." I smiled sweetly and moved from one leg to the other awkwardly. "I'm Jane Kingsley."

"Daxon. Daxon Rivera." He smirked down at me, bringing his fingers to the collar of my robe. "Did I interrupt something?" His thumb moved across the soft, plush fabric of the only clothing I was wearing. My breath caught in my throat as I fumbled around for an excuse.

"Um," I swallowed hard. "I was about to take a bath." Lying was never one of my specialties, which he quickly caught onto.

"After a performance like that, I'd assume you'd work up quite a sweat." He bit his lip to suppress a knowing smirk, his cheek indenting with a dimple. With my brain coming up blank on a response, my cheeks flushed with embarrassment.

"O-Oh, I-I-"

"Don't worry, I'm a big fan." He winked, stepping backward down the steps of my house's patio. "By the way, Princesa, I'd close your curtains from now on." The officer skipped down the stairs and down the sidewalk to the next house. My jaw was practically on the floor. Slamming the door, I ran to my room and pulled on some clothes.

My new neighbor saw me naked.

My new cop neighbor saw me naked.

Despite the temperature, I buried myself in the blankets of my bed, wanting to escape the deeply embedded embarrassment in my stomach. Vivian came home a few hours later, as promised. She disappeared into the kitchen, making her fresh fruit smoothies and preparing her organic-based dinner. Curtains now tied closed, I sauntered into the kitchen and sat at the table.

"What's for supper, Wifey?" I waggled my eyebrows at her playfully. Vivian smiled and shook her head, plating the food and placing it in front of me.

"Rosemary chicken with cherry salsa." She stuck a fork into the chicken breast and started plating her own food.

"What would I do without you?" I questioned, digging in. Viv was a culinary major and being her roommate backslash best friend, definitely had its perks. I debated on telling her about what happened with the new neighbor, but decided against it.

"Anything interesting happen while I was gone?" She questioned as she cut into her chicken. Biting my lip, I shook my head.

"Nope. Boring, like always."

2

CHAPTER 2

The next morning, I woke up to the sound of Vivian's melodic yoga music. Stumbling out of bed, I made my way past Viv's room where she was stretched into some kind of weird flexible move. Ending up in the bathroom, I made sure the curtains were closed before stripping off my pajamas and hopping in the shower. Because of the California heat, my showers were often on the cooler side, but nevertheless felt amazing against my tanned skin.

I worked at a bakery called 'Get Baked' before and after school, and on weekends to keep myself busy. Because I loved the smell of fresh baked goods, I always volunteered for the opening shift, but since the opening shift was at five AM, I rarely had any customers. I pulled on a pair of black leggings and the bakery's signature shirt with a big dopey looking muffin on the front.

"If you have any strawberry frosted doughnuts left over, bring me one back?" She batted her eyelashes at me and I rolled my eyes.

"I'll see you at school." I pulled on my white and black Adidas sneakers and shut the front door behind me. The drive to work was quiet, the only sound being the soft hum of the radio that was on its lowest volume. When I got to the bakery, I unlocked the door and turned on the lights. Display cases lit up, the kitchen illuminated and I set out to work. Dozens of muffins, cookies, and doughnuts were baking and frying within a half hour. I was frosting the last blueberry glazed doughnut when the entrance door jingled. "I'll be right with you!" I called from the kitchen, setting the doughnut down on a rack and wiping my hands on the apron I was wearing. "You're my first custom-"

There he was, in all his glory. Now wearing a pair of black jeans and a grey t-shirt that read 'Santa Ana PD,' Officer Rivera stood beautifully behind the counter. His green eyes were trained on me, a smirk on his lips.

"Good morning, Ms. Kingsley." He said slowly, his mouth wrapping against my surname sensually.

"M-Morning." I stuttered, my cheeks heating up again at the memory of our last talk. "What can I get yo-"

"I didn't peg you for someone who worked at a bakery." He interrupted, looking me up and down observantly. I frowned slightly, unintentionally crossing my arms over my chest. He noticed and chuckled. "Not that that's a bad thing, it's cute." My cheeks heated up again and I cursed him for having this affect on me.

"Well I didn't peg you for a pervert." I shot back, a small amount of confidence seeping through my coyness. He smirked; there was that dimple again. It was then I noticed his arms were fully tattooed into sleeves of art that danced across his skin.

"I like it when you're mouthy." He leaned against the counter, crossing his arms over his chest as well. My brow furrowed in frustration.

"What can I get you." I stated rather than questioned. He chuckled softly and looked through what I had put into the display cases. Biting his lip, he pointed to the doughnut rack.

"I'll have one apple fritter and one French cruller." I nodded and pulled out a bag, gently placing the two sweets inside.

"That'll be three dollars." I mumbled, avoiding his emerald colored eyes. He pulled out three bills and handed them over to me. "Thank you."

"Baking sweets fits you, Princesa." He whispered softly, taking the bag from my hand and softly running his thumb over my knuckles. "I can only imagine you taste just as sweet as your work." He turned and walked out of the shop, the loud jingle from the door leaving me feeling lonely.

My shift was over seven hours later and right on schedule, I pulled up to University California-Davis. My hands trembled nervously as I walked into my animal anatomy class, knowing a heavily weighted test was about to be given. I missed my mom at times like these, she always knew what to say when I was stressed. The professor ranted on about the importance of doing well and that this test could either make or break this semester's grade.

"Begin." He said gruffly, scooting into his desk and correcting our projects from last week. I started by writing my name neatly above the questions and then gulped at the sight of the lengthy test. Ten pages, back to back, of questions relating from the anatomy of goldfish to the anatomy of a horse. Glancing at the clock quickly, I bit my lip with the knowledge that I only had an hour to complete this.

I breezed through the dog and cat questions, because frankly, they were the easiest. It was easy to remember the anatomy of animals that actually interested you. I could have done without the cows, the birds, and the pigs. After I had finished, I hesitantly walked up to the professor's desk and handed in my test. When the last person had finished, he dismissed the class with annoyed wave. As I was walking out, someone gently tapped my shoulder.

"You're Jane, right?" I turned, finding a boy around my age with tousled dirty blonde hair. His blue eyes watched me playfully as I nodded in response. A few freckles peppered his deeply tanned skin, his toned arms sticking out from the loose royal blue tank he was wearing.

"I'm Riley. Marine animal veterinarian to be." He stuck his hand out to me and I shook it politely.

"Nice to meet you." I smiled softly and began to walk away before he caught my wrist.

"Sorry, it's just-" He paused, rethinking his word choice. "I've seen you around and I've seen how passionate you are about this. I guess I was just wondering if we could grab a coffee sometime?" He grimaced even before I replied, probably anticipating a rejection.

"Uh, yeah." I nodded, biting my lip. "What's your number, I'll message you when I'm free." After exchanging numbers, Riley and I parted ways. Riley was cute, polite, and sweet, which was everything I was looking for in a man. But somehow my mind wandered back to Officer Rivera and what he said.

"I can only imagine you taste just as sweet as your work."

What had he meant by that? I tried to talk myself into rationally believing he was a cannibal and was interested in me purely because I was his next victim. But I knew better and the worst part was, part of me wondered what he tasted like, too.

3

CHAPTER 3

Dropping the bag with the last strawberry frosted dough-nut from the bakery onto Vivian's bed, I went back to my room to study. Riley and I texted back and forth a few times, and I found myself giggling at his silly replies. Viv poked her head inside my room with offerings of chocolate and binge watching Netflix shows. And I finally spilled the beans; about Officer Rivera and most recently: Riley.

"He said that to you?" She gasped, her small, feminine fingers reaching up to cover her mouth in surprise. "That's so dirty."

"That's what I thought!" I threw my hands up, relieved I wasn't insane. Standing up, I walked over to the window and peeked out to the other side that faced the officer's house. "He says such seemingly innocent things, but they're laced with miles of sexual innuendo."

"Well, I think you need some stress relief; use him, abuse him, lose him." She winked, popping a piece of chocolate into her mouth.

"Yeah." I breathed out, knowing I wasn't capable of that kind of relationship.

"Let's get your mind off of this." She sprung up and marched over to our movie collection.

We sat on the couch watching Pretty Woman, Vivian was a huge fan of Julia Roberts. Each time it was rumored that she was in California, Vivian would drive hours to wherever the actress had been spotted. She reminded me of a young Julia Roberts sometimes, with her big smile and red hair.

"God, I love this part." She whispered, mouthing the dialogue, "You're late. You're stunning. You're forgiven." I laughed at her cheesiness, glad that the girl next to me was my best friend. My stomach growled with hunger and I stood, walking to the kitchen.

"Need anything? I'm going to make food." I called to her from the kitchen, pulling out a package of tortillas and a package of cheese. Quesadillas were one of my favorite snacks, cheese being my favorite thing period; nachos, cheese burgers, macaroni and cheese, pizza, grilled cheese - you name it.

"Grab the bag of M&M's!" She yelled back, returning to reciting the dialogue of the 1990 classic. I smiled and flipped the quesadilla over in the pan, hearing the excess cheese sizzle against the stainless steel. After it was done, I plated my food and grabbed the bag of M&M's before plopping back on the couch next to Vivian. "Thanks, Wifey." She smiled at me and ripped open the bag. After a few minutes, she looked at the clock and then to me.

"Is if awful that I'm still hungry?" I chuckled and shook my head.

"What're you in the mood for?" I questioned, grimacing as I wiggled the toes of one of my feet that had fallen asleep.

"Pizza." She gushed, throwing her head back in mock ecstasy. Smiling and shaking my head, I reached for my phone, but to my surprise, it wasn't on the coffee table. Frowning, I stood and jogged to my room, finding it on my pillow.

"How'd you get in here?" I mumbled, picking it up. My curiosity quickly changed subject as I noticed lights flash across my window. Tiptoeing to the window, I peeked through the curtain and watched as Officer Rivera stepped out of his black Camaro. The passenger side of the car opened and out stepped a gorgeous girl with flowing blonde hair. She wore a tight black dress and silver stilettos, wobbling up to the door behind the cop. A pang of an unfamiliar emotion boiled in my stomach, but I pushed it away to focus on watching the two go inside. Thankfully, the large windows in the officer's living room gave me the perfect opportunity to be a weirdo stalker.

The couple sat on the couch, sipping wine from glass flutes for a few minutes before she kissed him. Her hands found his hair, pulling and tugging at the dark brown locks as they explored each other. The officer's fingers dug into the woman's hips, pulling her into his awaiting lap. Her dress hiked, revealing a dark red thong which he spent little time ignoring. Holding onto her butt, Officer Rivera stood and laid her across his ottoman, slowly pulling her dress over her head.

"I should not be watching his." I whispered, fully aware that Vivian was in the next room waiting for me and I was being a huge creep. But I couldn't tear my eyes away; the woman now completely naked beside the heels still strapped to her feet. The officer pulled off his shirt, revealing his chiseled figure and defined abdomen. I bit my lip, my breath hitching in my throat as he slowly pulled his black jeans down and stepped out of them. The only thing between them was now the fabric of the cop's boxer briefs and I felt that familiar feeling run through me again.

And then our eyes met.

Officer Rivera's green eyes found mine through the window, catching me watching him with this woman. His lips cocked into a smirk and he slowly pulled his boxers down. Keeping my eyes locked with his, he entered her and I could hear her moans even from where I stood. I swallowed hard, his eyes not leaving mine as he pulled out and thrust back into her. The woman clawed his back with her French tipped nails, obviously enjoying her time with my neighbor despite his attention now on me. A thick sheen of sweat spread over his back as he flipped her over onto her hands and knees, entering her from behind. I gasped, feeling a certain warmth awaken in my core. He bit his lip and wrapped his fingers around her long hair, pulling it to force the woman's spine to arch and slammed into her backside relentlessly. By the look on her face, it was more than pleasing.

"Hey, did you fall asleep or something?" Vivian called from the living room and I broke out of my trance. My cheeks heated as I whipped my curtains closed and ran back to my best friend's side. "Jeez, are you okay?" She questioned, noticing my heavy breathing and flushed face.

"Uh, yeah." I shook my head, pulling up the Domino's app on my phone. "What toppings do you want?"

4

— ◦ —

CHAPTER 4

I avoided any and all contact from my next door neighbor. Every time he walked outside, I conveniently had something to do inside. When he busied himself by washing his car shirt-less, I buried myself in homework. It was like I was in this never ending cycle of lust toward him and it needed to stop. He was cocky and arrogant; everything I was trying to stay away from, but somehow, it allured me even further.

To keep my mind off of the cop, I made plans with Riley. Since I rarely ever go out, Viv happily helped me put together an out-fit, do my hair, and apply my makeup. With a red wine colored off-shouldered mini dress, dark brown curled hair down the length of my spine, and winged eyeliner, Vivian sent me off into Riley's waiting car. As I pulled open the door of Riley's Jeep, I made eye contact with Officer Rivera as he sat on his patio with a beer bottle in hand. Feeling a rush of embarrassment, I quickly jumped into the car and buckled myself up.

On the way to the restaurant, Riley was a complete gen-tlemen. He asked how comfortable I was, if I need the car's temperature hotter or cooler, and how the hell I'm so damn pretty. When we pulled up to the five star establishment, I bit my lip.

"We don't have to go here, I heard this place is wicked expensive." I watched as he shook his head with an amused grin, jogging over to the passenger's side of the car and opening the door for me.

"Let's just say, I have an in with the owner." He winked and we walked inside, past the line of hungry waiting restaurant-goers. We were seated in a private room in the back; the walls a lavish red, gold fixtures and table settings, mahogany wood flooring, and a live jazz band that played softly in the background. "Riley, you didn't have to do all of this for me." I insisted, but he shook his head again.

"You're special, Jane. Anyone with half a brain can see that." He shot me a charming smile and I, quite honestly, nearly melted. Having long forgotten the cop next door, I ordered the fettuccine with a side of broiled asparagus in a garlic butter sauce while Riley splurged on a twelve ounce steak and a side of rosemary-infused mashed potatoes. My date was everything a girl could hope for; smart, funny, easy-going, and goal oriented. "I have a job lined up after graduation at a private marine animal hospital." I took a sip of the wine Riley had chosen for us, my mouth swirling with hints of rich earthiness and a sweet after taste. "Good, isn't it? It's a 2008 Littorai Thieriot Vineyard Chardonnay." I nodded pleasingly.

"I don't usually drink, but this is amazing." I smiled, setting the glass back down.

"Well, Jane," Riley folded his hands together and set them on the table in front of him, eyeing me with a curious expression. "We've sat here talking about my life, school, and the weather for about forty-five minutes and you haven't told me a lick about you."

"Yeah, sorry about that. I'm awful at first dates and I hate talking about myself." I gushed, knowing that first dates had always been a weakness of mine. "What would you like to know?"

"Where are you from?" He asked, cutting into his medium-rare steak.

"A little town in Wisconsin, a couple hour from Milwaukee."

"When did you meet Vivian?" I blushed as I thought back to Vivian giving Riley the "parent talk" and supplying me with a tube of pepper spray.

"Have her home at a decent hour and if you hurt her, I will hunt you down and rip your dick off."

"We've been friends since diapers; she packed up her whole life to move here with me, I owe her everything." I said honestly, feeling my love for my best friend resonate throughout the small room.

"She seems great, it must be nice to have someone like that in your life." He replied, popping a piece of tender meat into his mouth.

"You don't?" I questioned, taking a bite of my own food. God, this was fricken good.

"After high school, I kind of just put my all into studying and passing college that I lost touch with a lot of my friends." He shrugged, "But I just see it as an opportunity to move forward and make new ones." That was one thing I really liked about Riley: he was always so optimistic. "Anyway, what does your family think of the move? Don't they miss you?"

This was the question I had been waiting for all night.

"Um, no." I shook my head, a lump forming in my throat. "They died a year and a half ago." Riley paled, quickly taking my hand in his and giving it a gentle squeeze.

"Damn it, I'm so sorry. I didn't know-"

"You couldn't have, it's okay." I smiled reassuringly, pushing back the tears that wanted to pour out of my eyelids. "But I'd like to think they miss me." Riley's embarrassed expression turned to one of sympathy, his thumb running over the lines on my palm.

"I'm sure they do."

He quickly changed the subject to my favorite food and I was thankful, finally letting go of the breath I had been holding. At the end of our meal, the waiter that had been assigned to our table handed over the check to Riley.

"Thank you, Colin." He opened the fold and took out the receipt, signing the small piece of paper before handing it back to the waiter.

"Will there be anything else, Sir?" Colin asked Riley, but he shook his head.

"No, but please tell my parents to order more of the Littorai Thieriot Vineyard Chardonnay." The waiter nodded and walked back to the kitchen, but my jaw had hit the hardwood floor.

"Your family owns this place?" I whispered in disbelief. Riley chuckled and nodded, standing before helping me out of my own chair.

"It doesn't take much to impress you, Jane." He said, amused at my reaction.

"Says the guy whose family owns a restaurant that has chains all over the world." I smacked his arm playfully and he opened my car door, helping me inside. The ride back to my house was short, but nonetheless lively as Riley told stories of his parent's rise to success. When we pulled up to my house, Riley walked me to my door.

This was the tough part: to kiss or not to kiss?

The blonde man in front of me lifted his hand and gently trailed his thumb along my cheekbone and my eyelids fluttered shut.

Yes, please kiss me.

Taking the hint, Riley slowly leaned in and pressed his soft lips to my own. His fingers cupped my cheek while his teeth softly grazed my lower lip. Parting my lips, I waited eagerly for more before a loud bang interrupted the moment. Riley and

I both turned to watch my neighbor exit his home and lean against the railing of his patio, his eyes on us but somehow his demeanor seemed hostile. His hands were balled into fists, eyebrows furrowed, and muscles constricting under his tight plain white v-neck tee.

"I guess that's my cue." Riley laughed awkwardly, letting his back face the cop that lived next door to me. I smiled apologetically and kissed his cheek.

"I had a really nice time tonight." I whispered, my hand now on the front door's knob. Riley's face lit up at my words and he nodded.

"Me too, I'll call you later." He leaned forward and pressed a gentle kiss to my forehead. "Goodnight."

"Goodnight." I waved as he got back into his car and drove off. I leaned dreamily against my front door, my fingertips brushing across my lips in remembrance of Riley's kiss. But then I remembered the perv who sat on his patio, still watching me. I quickly pulled out my keys, fumbling to find the right one before he spoke.

"You know, Princesa," He leaped from his patio and pulled himself onto my front porch. My heart jumped into my throat, my palms becoming slick with sweat. His arm were now on either sides of me, trapping me between them as he looked down at me with his emerald gaze. "I have a feeling you've been avoiding me."

"I have." I shot back, my embarrassment taking a turn into anger for having ruined my first kiss with Riley.

"Why is that?" He questioned, his lips now just milometers from mine.

Fucking kiss me. I thought at him. No, Jane, stop it!

"Stop it, Dax." I wouldn't meet his eyes, I couldn't. His hot breath trailed up my neck, his soft lips ghosting over the exposed flesh. He chuckled when my back arched involuntarily, my cheeks flaring hot and pink.

"It's Officer Rivera, to you." His deep voice rasped quietly in my ear. "Besides, you don't want me to stop, Princesa."

"If you don't stop, I'll-"

"You'll what?" He interrupted, smirking against my jawline. "Call the police?"

I gasped softly and ducked under his arms, quickly unlocking my door and slipping inside. Leaving the sexually charged officer on my doorstep, I leaned against the door and slowly slid down.

What the hell is going on?

5

CHAPTER 5

The next morning before work, I received a bright orange envelope on my doorstep. With my coffee in hand, I picked it up and noticed it was addressed to me, from Santa Ana PD. A frown instantly formed on my face as I ripped open the letter and read the print.

Defendant: Jane Elisa KingsleyAge: 21 years (10/31/1996)Time of Citation: 3:02 AMViolation: Public Nudity/Indecent ExposureCode: 314 PCOfficer: 414 / Daxon Rivera

His signature finalized the citation and my blood boiled at the sight.

"Are you freaking kidding me?" I screamed, not caring if I woke Vivian. I dropped my coffee and ran across my yard into his, marching up the steps of his patio and banging on his front door. "Open up, Rivera! I know you're in there!" The door gingerly opened to reveal a very sleepy, very shirtless officer groggily looking at me with a slight smirk.

"Good morning, Ms. Kingsley." He spoke, his voice deeper and more rasp from having just been woken up. God was he sexy... Wait, no.

"What the hell is this?" I threw the orange paper at him and he read it over.

"Hm," He looked over the print thoughtfully. "Oh, yes. This is the ticket I left on your doorstep."

"No way!" I gasped sarcastically. "I'm just wondering why." He leaned against the door frame, a cocky smile on his lips.

"Go out with me." My eyes nearly fell out of my head, my heartbeat thundering in my chest.

"No!" I yelled, poking his chest. "You gave me a bogus ticket! This better not be going on my record, I will fight this in court-"

"It's fake." He interjected, still smiling despite my rejecting him. "So is that a hard no, or...?" He asked teasingly, leaning forward slightly to catch me off guard.

"Hard as freaking rock." I hissed before turning on my heel to leave. The officer quickly wrapped his fingers around my wrist and pulled me back to him, our chests now flush against each other.

"Then lets be friends." He whispered, his minty breath hitting my lips. I bit my own, feeling the familiar urge to get rid of the space between us.

"O-Okay.." I stuttered, pushing some space between us. "But that means no flirting, no pushing personal boundaries-"

"No looking into the other's window when they're fucking a girl they brought home." Dax smirked, winking cheekily. Blood rushed to my cheeks and I shook my head, walking down the stairs of his patio. "Wait!" He caught me again and frowned.

"I'm sorry, I was just joking." I rolled my eyes and continued walking. "Where are you going?"

"School." I answered bluntly, pulling my front door open.

"So... Friends?" He called over to me.

"Friends."

"And just like that, no more sexy talk?" Vivian pouted, walking me to my final class for the day. I shrugged, my eyes finding Riley who had saved a seat for me next to him.

"That what he said, and honestly I'm relieved. Now I can focus on other things." I smiled hopefully, holding my books to my chest like a giddy school girl. Viv rolled her eyes and followed my gaze to Riley.

"Other things like animal-loving surfer boy in there?" She questioned, her hands now on her hips. My grin gave me away as I waved her goodbye and entered the classroom. I took my seat next to Riley and he leaned over to press a kiss to my cheek. A deep blush consumed my cheeks as I watched several people look our way.

"Sorry, I couldn't resist." He chuckled, pulling out his laptop.

"People are staring." I whispered, looking around me at the girls who were starring daggers into my head. Riley wrapped his arm around my shoulders and leaned into his seat.

"Don't worry about it. They're just the background, all that matters is right here." He mumbled into my ear as the professor started to teach. The class went on just as normal, except for Riley and I playing footsie under our desks. When the lights came back on prior to taking notes off of the projector, I collected my things and stuffed them into my backpack. "Hey, I'll carry that for you." Riley said, pulling one strap of my backpack over his shoulder. Smiling in thanks, we walked to my car and he slipped my things into the passenger seat.

"So the guy, your neighbor, from last night-"

"We're friends. Just friends." I blurted out quickly causing him to laugh.

"Don't worry, Jane, I trust you." He slipped a few strands of hair behind my ear. "I just need to know if it's something I need to worry about."

"Absolutely not."

When I got home, I set my things on my dresser and slumped into my bed. The past couple weeks had really hit me hard. The feeling of my favorite pajama set had my body aching for a much needed slumber. But then, almost as if I was being punished, someone knocked at the door. I trudged to the front door and opened it to reveal Officer Friendly.

"Evening, Gorgeous." He winked, dressed in a pair of dark blue jeans and a black v-neck. "Get dressed." He pushed past me and entered my room as if he'd done it a million times before. His fingers breezed through my closet before settling on a pair of light-wash skinny jeans and my old Rolling Stones t-shirt.

"What're you doing?" I questioned from the doorway, utterly confused.

"We're going out."

6

— • —

Chapter 6

"**A** biker bar?" I stood in disbelief at the neon lights that read 'Wheels & Heels.' Daxon slapped his large hand against my back in a friendly gesture, pushing me forward and through the front door.

"Yup," He said, popping the consonant. "And there's an open booth." I slid into the beat up leather seating and pulled the menu to my eye level. "This place is a hidden gem; they've got the best food in the city." I nodded as my eyes took in the greasy, cheesy goodness. The waitress came to our table and instantly drank in the sight of Dax.

"What can I give you?" Her large bust popped out of her half-unbuttoned top and she leaned forward to use it on Dax.

"Scotch, neat; and I'd like a the double cheeseburger with extra bacon." He set the menu down and nodded toward me, as if the waitress was invisible.

"Same as him." I gave her my menu and watched as she left, wagging her hips dramatically from side to side. Snorting, my eyes finally met with his. Dax's lips tipped into a slight smirk.

"What?" I asked self-consciously, squirming under his gaze.

"You just fascinate me." He said, his accent laced with each word that came from his mouth. I found myself watching his lips and I looked away, feeling my cheeks heat.

"Why is that?" I kept my eyes anywhere but the man in front of me; the friend in front of me. Dax folded his hands in front of himself and leaned forward.

"Come close," He insisted, wagging his index finger at me. Leaning in, my fists quickly clenched under the table as I felt his hot breath against my ear. God, his cologne was incredible.

"You have so much... self control. Something I have little of." He admitted, my breath now caught in my throat. I gulped to regain some composure, knowing his words were embedded with sexual undertones. He leaned back against his seat and smiled innocently at my exasperated expression.

"Well," I bit my lip. "You should work on that." He shrugged effortlessly and smiled thankfully at the waitress as she brought our drinks to the table.

"I find self control to be a restraint." He said thoughtfully, taking a small drink from his glass. "God knows I like to be in control." Another wave of heat past through me, but instead of it coming to my cheeks, it resonated in my core. I crossed my legs slowly and attempted to change the subject.

"How was your day?" How lame, Jane.

"Rough." He admitted, drinking the entirety of his drink at the sound of the topic. "I can't really talk about the details, but I had a domestic violence call; the girl didn't make it." Suddenly, my mood shifted and I found myself reaching over the table to grab his hand to comfort him.

"I'm sorry, I know the feeling of seeing someone die." My heart clenched. "It's an awful thing to go through." Dax stayed quiet, so I continued. "My parents... they were killed in a home invasion last year." When his eyes lifted to me and I knew his expression well. It was one I had seen many times; at their funeral, at school, anywhere someone knew my family. "Viv and I moved here for a fresh start." I waited a moment for the 'I'm so sorry for your loss' speech, but Dax did something that surprised me.

"This song is nice." He mumbled and I strained to hear the foreign music over the bustle of the other bar-goers.

"I don't understand it." I bit my lip, feeling embarrassed that I couldn't recollect any of my high school Spanish.

"It's okay, Princesa, I can translate." He held out his hand to me. My palm met his and he whisked me into the center of the bar where his free hand rested on my hip. Pulling me close, he moved to the slow beat of the song, leading me with ease. "This song is about a man who is desperately in love and wishes to be with his love because his life isn't worth living without her." He whispered softly to me, my forehead lazily leaning against his hard chest as we danced, his warmth enveloping me in a cocoon of bliss. The heartache of the loss of my parents had been forgotten thanks to Dax's distraction and I made note of his dancing expertise.

"And it would be an honor, oh love, to be your slave! would become your toy by my own willAnd if a glorious day I end up in your armsThat would be happiness-"

He translated to me quietly and I looked up at him quizzically.

"Why would you want to be a slave to someone?" Dax shrugged and I felt his thumb trace small circles into my hip.

"People do odd things when they are in love." He looked down at me, his eyes hard with seriousness.

"I wouldn't know," I blurted honestly. "I've never been in love." That seemed to please Dax and he pulled away, twirling me in a circle before bringing me back into his chest.

"Tell me something about Jane." He smiled a charming smile. "As your friend, I'm obligated to know you inside and out." I rolled my eyes.

"I'm boring-"

"I know that's not true." He bit his lip to stop himself from laughing. "By day: a baker at your local bakery, but by night: ...a Sir Mix-a-Lot impersonator." He wiggled his eyebrows playfully. I swatted his chest.

"Shut up!"

"But seriously, tell me something interesting." He chuckled and I searched my brain.

"I've never been to a club and I love to cook and bake." I spouted out, realizing the song had ended minutes ago and somehow we were still embraced. Taking a step away, I

scratched the back of my head awkwardly. "Our food is here."
I rushed to the table and took my seat, digging into the thick
cheeseburger in front of me.

"Damn." Dax chuckled, watching me devour the food before
he had even taken a bite.

"Oh, yeah." I giggled, looking down at my plate. "I love to eat."
He started on his own food and smiled softly.

"I like a woman who can eat."

"Don't all women eat?" I questioned sarcastically. He nodded, wiping the grease off of his hands with a napkin.

"Yeah, but the women I'm typically around pretend to eat like
birds." He popped a French fry into his mouth before continuing. "It's refreshing to see such a small girl have such a big
appetite." My cheeks heated for the millionth time and I quietly
finished my food. The ride home was filled with music from the
radio, but we didn't talk. And for some reason, we didn't need
to. Dax walked me to the middle of the sidewalk that separated
our houses, stuffing his hands in his jean pockets. "Thanks for
distracting me from work stuff."

"I had fun." I replied honestly, rocking back and forth on my
heels.

"Good." He mumbled. And for once, it seemed like Daxon
Rivera wasn't sure of what to say.

"Goodnight." I waved and turned to walk to my house.

"Goodnight, Princesa." He said from behind me. Once in my bedroom, I finally pulled out my phone and noticed a message from Riley.

R- Hey, babe. Just got home from the gym. Do anything interesting tonight?

I paused before replying.

J- Went to dinner with a friend.

7

⸺ ✦ ⸺

CHAPTER 7

With only my finals left to complete the summer classes I was in, I shut myself into my room for days trying to study. Vivian occasionally popped her head in to give me a mental break, filling me in on the outside world. A stench began to fester from my clothes due to my lack of showering, but that seemed less of a priority at the moment. Riley had disappeared into his own studying meltdown, leaving me to suffer alone binge-reading textbooks with a plate of chicken nuggets at my side.

Hearing the front door open and close was something I had come to ignore. Viv was always in and out, I didn't bother keeping track anymore. My bedroom door creaked open slowly, but I didn't look up as I replied, finding even a millisecond of wasted time to be earth-shattering. The springs of my bed shifted with weight and I sighed.

"I can't really talk right now, Viv-"

"Good thing I'm not Viv." His deep voice chuckled. I whipped around, facing the dark-haired officer himself. He smirked at me from my bed, sporting a pair of dark-washed jeans and a plain white v-neck tank.

"What're you doing here?" I quickly turned away to stop staring at the flecks of water dripping from his hair. Must've just gotten out of the shower...

"Bored." He shrugged, grabbing a stuffed Beluga whale I had gotten from Sea World when I was four. "Besides, it'd been a few days since I saw my Princesa." A thought crossed my mind to correct the use of his possessive my, but part of me felt comforted even thrilled by it.

"Oh." I replied simply, biting my lip and going back to reading. Dax stayed quiet, but I could feel his heated gaze on the back of my matted-haired head. Suddenly feeling self conscious, I shifted in my desk chair and looked up at the ceiling.

"You may as well go, I'm no fun right now. I've been up for nearly forty-eight hours studying with no end in sight."

"Let me help you." He stood, grabbing the beanbag chair from the corner of my room and throwing it beside me. Plopping down, he grabbed my textbook and I watched his eyes skim over the content. "Give an example of a Dorsal on a dog."

"The backbone is a Dorsal to the dog's stomach." I shook my head. "Dax, you don't have to do this-"

"I want to." He smiled promisingly. "Now, true or false: a dog's spleen is roughly the same size as its stomach and lies near it." We studied for hours, only breaking to grab a drink or heat up more nuggets. To my surprise, studying with a partner made the process go far faster. At the end of the fourth hour Dax had helped me, I slumped in my chair.

"Thank you." I breathed in relief, a weight lifted from my shoulders knowing I had studied my butt off. Quite literally, my butt had fallen asleep with all the sitting I had done.

"You don't have to thank me-" Standing and stretching my limbs to their longest capacity, I watched Dax's eyes flicker to the sliver of skin that showed between my pajama shorts and my shirt that had risen with my movements. "We're friends."

"Seriously though, Dax," I turned away from him, feeling my cheeks heat. "What we covered in four hours, I would've cover in eight on my own." The beanbag crumpled under his weight as he stood, approaching from behind me. My breath caught slightly as I felt his breath on my skin, starting from my exposed collarbones and fanning up my neck. "D-Dax-" His name stuck in my throat, large hands engulfing my waist between them. Thoughts began to cloud my mind, bad thoughts. "Dax, I'm gross right now..."

"You are beautiful, Jane." And for some reason, hearing my name fall from his lips, caused my panties to flush. His lips ghosted over my skin causing goosebumps to rise on the surface. Swallowing hard, I found myself craning my neck to the side for more. His lips now at my jaw, I bit my lip in painful anticipation. As if he had a GPS for my body, he found the sweet spot just below my ear and I moaned softly.

"Dax..." I mumbled, stumbling on every letter because my brain had checked out for the evening.

"Louder." He growled, his fingers digging into my hips.

"Da-"

Bing

My phone chirped from my desk and we froze and in that moment, feeling caught in the midst of our heated moment. And then reality dawned.

"Oh my god." I gasped, pulling away quickly and throwing my arms around myself. "I'm with Riley, I'm his girlfriend - we are dating. I shouldn't be..." Daxon stared blankly at me, a look of indifference plaguing his normally beautiful features. "I'm tired and not thinking clearly-"

"I'm sure that's what it was." He said blandly, his tone laced with sarcasm.

"Dax, stop it." I frowned, pacing the floor of my bedroom. "What do I tell Riley?"

"Don't." He shrugged, leaning coolly against the wall. I snorted in disgust.

"Oh, okay!" I threw my hands up in frustration. "What if your girlfriend had done something like this-"

"I don't have a girlfriend." He licked the corner of his lips and I shivered.

"Hypothetically." I grit, becoming furious at his lack of empathy.

"Hypothetically; if I had a girlfriend, I'd fuck her. I'd fuck her every single day, any chance she'd allow. I'd worship her body, pray to whatever higher power is out there in thanks for her beautiful creation. She wouldn't have the leg strength to walk her ass anywhere after I'm done with her, much less mess around with another guy." His response had taken me aback, so much that we stared at each other in silence. After several moments filled with thick, uncomfortable quietness, I found a minuscule amount of confidence.

"I think you should leave." I whispered, my eyes glued to the floor. He opened his mouth to say something, but snapped it shut. I turned away as he walked out of my bedroom and slammed the front door behind him.

8

CHAPTER 8

Daxon

It'd been over a week since I'd last spoken to her. I had no reason to be pissed; she was right, she's got a boyfriend and I should respect that. But I couldn't help but be a little distant. I was struggling enough with keeping something so big from her, living next to her, and stupidly being attracted to her. In an attempt to make myself feel better about the situation, I tried to convince myself that I was so unbelievably into her because I couldn't have her. She's untouchable.

But that wasn't stopping me for whatever reason.

Every time I was near her, my self control withered away almost instantaneously. My usual resolved nature became something animalistic and territorial whenever I saw her near that skinny little blonde of a boyfriend. Being the honest person that I am, I am big enough to say I'm the jealous type. Considering Jane and I are not even together, there is something undoubtedly wrong with me.

I walked out of my house, swinging my key ring around my index finger as I whistled on the way to my car. The Camaro beeped when I unlocked it, echoing in the quietness of the early morning. From next door, Jane popped out of her house and hopped down the stairs dressed in a pair of black spandex shorts and a light blue athletic tank top. I sucked my lip between my teeth and shoved my sunglasses on to hide my wandering eyes. Upon seeing me, she gave an awkward wave and a sheepish smile. Nodding in response, I hopped into the driver's seat and jolted the car to life. My foot, suddenly plagued with lead, forcibly pushed on the gas pedal and I pulled the shift into reverse. Shooting out of my driveway, I caught a glance of Jane in my review mirror and frowned, seeing the shocked expression on her face mold into hurt.

In hope of distracting myself, I blasted the radio through the speaker system and drummed my index fingers against the steering wheel. The short drive to work ended as I pulled into my assigned spot. Kicking the door closed, I shoved my keys into the pocket of my black jeans and walked into the station. The smell of disinfectant and coffee wafted my senses immediately. Officer Will Perez approached me, wearing yellow cleaning gloves up the length of his arms and holding a spray bottle filled with cleaning chemicals. Pulling the paper mask away from his face, he set the bottle down and stripped off the gloves.

"Knife fight on the boardwalk; Anderson brought the two in and put them in separate holding cells, but there was blood everywhere," He pulled out a pack of gum and popped it into his mouth. "You just missed it." Slapping him on the shoulder, I smiled sarcastically.

"Lucky me." I made my way past reception and toward my desk, but not before Blake stopped me. The perky blonde had made it her top priority to try to sleep with me and despite her efforts, never made it in my pants. Feeling her skinny, manicured fingers grasp the bottom of my bicep made me sigh in annoyance.

"Good morning Chief Inspector." She beamed, tugging me slightly in the direction of her desk. "I brought in doughnuts for everyone, why don't you have one?"

"Morning, Blake and uh, no thanks." I shrugged my arm out of her grip, "Any messages?" She scrambled to her desk and pulled a pink sticky note from her stationary.

"Just one from Director General Ellis." She slid the note into my hand, giving it a gentle squeeze before making her way back to her desk. Rolling my eyes, I entered my office and shut the door behind me. I slid into my chair and looked down at the note, scribbled and dotted with small hearts.

Call me ASAP. -Director Ellis

Sighing softly with a little apprehension, I dialed my boss's number and for the first time in all of my career, he answered immediately.

"Rivera, we've got a problem." He spat into the phone and I grimaced, feeling my pulse quicken.

"What would be the problem, Sir." I questioned, tapping my foot anxiously against the metal of my desk leg.

"Dorian Smith broke out of prison late last night." My throat seized, my brain unable to formulate any words to respond. "He killed four guards and took another prisoner hostage to negotiate his escape. We have rescued the hostage, but Smith did manage to get away." I stayed silent, still unable to process the information coming at me. "Rivera."

"Yes, Sir." I mumbled into the receiver, all of the blood draining from my face as Jane popped into my mind.

"I realize you are close to this case so I'm assigning you to head this project," As Director Ellis continued to give me the run down of the situation, my eyes landed on the take-out bag from Jane's bakery and my fingers clenched into fists. No matter what was going to happen, Jane was going to be safe, and that I was sure of.

An hour later, I was in uniform and driving down Ophelia Avenue with Officer Perez in the passenger seat. Silence encapsulated the car to no end, but that was the least of my worries. As we pulled into Jane and Vivian's driveway, my heartbeat sped up erratically. Will gave me a sympathetic look as I took a deep breath and stepped out. We approached the door and I hesitated before knocking my knuckles against the wood.

"It'll be okay, Dax. I'm sure she'll understand." Will stated, and as much as I needed to hear that, I said nothing. The door opened and her face lit up with excitement.

"Dax!" She threw her arms around my torso and hugged me tightly. "I'm sorry about last week, okay? Can we just go back to how it was before?" She pulled away with a sad smile on her face before noticing my demeanor. "Is everything okay?" She looked between Will and me.

"Ms. Kingsley, Officer Perez and I are here in reference to a case you were involved in last year." I watched as her face began to pale.

"Jane, what's going on?" Vivian appeared behind the small brunette, resting a hand on her shoulder.

"I don't know." She whispered.

"Ms. Kingsley," I took a deep breath before finding the courage to say the words. "Dorian Smith escaped from Supermax late last evening and enforcement were unable to apprehend him." Jane was silent for a long time.

"Jane, isn't that-"

"The man who murdered my parents." And before anyone could react, Jane knees gave out and she dropped to the ground unconscious.

9

— • —

CHAPTER 9

Jane

My eyes were blurry with sleep from having been woken up by a call from the police department about an accident at my parent's house. My and Vivian's sleepover was officially disrupted and I could tell that her parents were less than over-joyed having been woken up by us tumbling down the stairs to get into my old red pickup truck and speed to my house. Viv was in the passenger seat spewing out words of comfort.

"Jay, it's going to be fine. I'm sure it's nothing." She smiled soothingly and I nodded in feigned agreement. Blue and red lights lit up the front lawn. Several men in uniform patrolled my family home and the land surrounding it. My eyes found the ambulance and it was as if my heart leaped into my throat. Without turning the truck off, I hopped out onto the gravel driveway and ran to the medical emergency vehicle.

"Oh my god." I cried out, watching as the paramedic zipped up the body bag, concealing my father's lifeless face. To afraid that I would scream, I covered my mouth with my hand and sunk into Vivian's awaiting arms.

"Hold shit." She whispered under her breath. A sob racked my body, rendering me completely helpless until a thought popped into my head.

Mom.

"Where's my mother?" I croaked to the paramedic, tears staining my cheeks raw and red.

"Other ambulance." He answered as he scribbled sentences down on a clipboard. Viv and I scrambled to the second ambulance where my mother's body was seizing, her face pale and distorted while her mouth gurgled out a foaming liquid. Paramedics surrounded her body until they finally stabilized her.

"She's lost a lot of blood, even if we were to make it to the hospital in time, she wouldn't make it." The lead paramedic put a hand on my shoulder to console me. "I'm sorry." I approached my mother's barely breathing body and I looked down at her trembling hands. Tears flooded my eyes but I quickly wiped them away; I needed to remember my last moments with my mother.

"Mom, I'm here." I whispered, pushing stray hair away from her face. The mother I had idolized as a child was gone, a ghost left in her absence. The woman in front of me was sickly pale, bloody, eyes glazed over and dead. "Mom, I love you." I kissed her cold knuckles as I tried to choke out the words. "I'm sorry

I wasn't here. I'm so sorry." Vivian hugged me from behind as I cried, watching my mother's chest rise for the last time before she slipped away. There was a tap on my shoulder, but I was too empty, too shocked to care, much less turn around.

"Ms. Kingsley, I am the lead detective assigned to this case, we have apprehended the perpetrator." I said nothing in response to the Spanish-accented man. "Do you need arrangements for somewhere to stay?"

"No, she can stay with me." Vivian interjected. I was numb and I was alone.

I stared shell-shocked, tears welling in my eyes. It took me so long to force those thoughts and feelings of that night out of my memory, and in one instant they came swarming back. Vivian was in the kitchen making tea, the two officers sat across from me on the opposite couch of my living room. My hands trembled as Vivian handed me the hot mug of Chamomile and honey, but I forced the liquid down my throat anyway.

"Ms. Kingsley, we're doing everything in our power to apprehend the perp-"

"Wait." I interrupted Dax as he spoke. "You." I pointed at him, the pieces of my memory slowly connected at the sound of his voice. "You were there." He wouldn't look at me, his eyes glued to the wall.

"I'm sorry, I'm confused." Vivian stated as she looked between Dax and me.

"You were there that night, weren't you?" I whispered, staring blankly at him. He turned his head away to avoid my gaze. "Look at me." A minute passed and he hadn't move. "Look at me, Dax."

"Ms. Kingsley, there's a lot to this case-" The other officer tried to save Dax.

"Yes, okay? I was the lead on your parent's case." Dax interrupted, throwing his hands up.

"That was in Wisconsin, why are you here? Why are you in California?" I shouted, anger crawling over my skin. "Were you following me?"

"Yes." He replied bluntly, facing me with indifference.

"Why." I choked out, my heart feeling betrayed and stupid.

"My commanding officer thought it best that I watch over you for a period of time, in case a situation like our current one would arise." He looked down at the officer beside him. "Let's go."

"Don't you dare leave." I spat, my fingers now formed into fists. "You owe me answers."

"I don't owe you anything, Jane. I was following orders." Dax said as he turned to leave.

"So that's all it was; just orders you were following?" I croaked, remembering the moment we had shared in my room last week. "It was all fake?" He stopped, facing away from me before spinning on his heel.

"What do you want from me, Jane? Huh?" He took another step forward, minimizing the space between us by half. "Do you want me to say that I came here on an assignment? Okay, fine. I did. If you're so committed to Riley, then why the hell are you so hurt that I lied?"

I said nothing.

"What the fuck do you want from me, Jane?" He took another step closer, I could feel his warmth and it soothed me. "Do you want me to tell you everything was a lie?" I looked up at him, his eyes watering. "Because it wasn't." He took my hands in his and shook his head. "I may have came here because I was assigned to, but goddammit, Jane, that's not why I stayed. I could've left weeks ago."

"Dax, I-"

The door opened and slammed closed, Riley appearing behind Dax.

"Babe, I'm so sorry I'm late." He pushed past Dax to pull me into a tight hug and I watched as Dax's head fell. Nodding, he sniffled and turned, walking out of the front door.

10

CHAPTER 10

My contact with Dax was few and far between. Knowing my schedule so well, he'd call about information on my case while I was at work or during my busy times of the day. He was playing phone tag and winning. But ever since Riley had become aware of my situation with the escaped convict that I shared a link to, he'd spent all of his free time with me. I loved that he cared so much about my safety, but part of me felt like I couldn't breathe.

"Do you want anything to eat?" Riley called from the kitchen of his inner-city apartment that he shared with his two room-mates.

"I'm okay, thanks." I said, flipping a page in the romance novel I had started.

There was no other woman for me. She was everything. The wind, the soil, the sun. Her voice was like liquid gold against my eardrum. But alas, as the closer to loving me she grew, the more she would grow further. I tried to love her slowly, I tried to love her fast. But she never loved me to the end - her heart belonged to another.

Riley popped something into the microwave before plopping down on the couch cushion beside me. I smiled gently before my eyes returned to the words on the pages in front of me.

"I know I've been a little overbearing..." Riley chuckled, biting his lip softly.

"No..." I said, a little too unconvincingly as I watched him grimace.

"I just really care about you, Janie. We've been going out for two months now and I feel sure enough of myself, of us, to say this and mean it-"

"Riley..."

"I love you, Janie." He took my hand in his. "You don't have to say it back yet, I just thought you should know, especially when so much is going on in your life right now." My stomach twisted and turned at his words. We sat in silence for awhile. "Say something. Please." He fiddled with his fingers in his lap. My heart clenched.

"I really care about you Riley, that means so much to me." I pulled him into a tight hug, burying my face in the crook of his neck. His arms slowly wrapped around me, his thumb rubbing softly against the exposed skin below my lifted shirt. Riley pulled me into his lap, my legs now cradling his waist as he continued to rub my back. Closing my eyes, I sighed in comfort, feeling almost sleepy. Suddenly his hand lifted, trailing up the length of my spine until it landed on my baby blue Nike sports bra. His fingers first smoothed over the fabric before attempting to slip inside. Something inside me snapped and I jumped to the other side of the couch.

"Um, Riley-" I breathed, my hands shaking. "I can't." Riley's jaw clenched for a moment before he nodded.

"Okay," He mumbled, looking at the clock suddenly. "I'll take you home." The car ride was silent; neither of us speaking until he pulled up in front of my house. "I'll call you later." He said, staring straight ahead at the road. I nodded and silently left the vehicle. His car sped away and I felt relieved with his absence. Without realizing, my head automatically turned to my neighbor's home. Dax came into view as he stepped out of his car. Black hair slicked back, tattoo covered muscles showing from the grey v-neck tee he was wearing, lips in a furrowed straight line. A woman followed suit, silky black hair falling down the length of her back, long jean clad legs and a white blouse fitted to every curve of her body. She was breathtaking. My heart seemed to plummet as I watched the pair turn to the sight of me.

"U-Uh, hey." I waved awkwardly, biting my lip. Dax looked between the girl and me, obviously unsure of what to do. The woman's eyes were dark brown and warm, her tanned skin glowing in the sunlight of the afternoon.

"Hola, mi nombre es-" The girl began to speak.

"Jane, this is-" Dax put his hand on the woman's shoulder and I flinched.

"It's fine, I get it." I smiled halfheartedly. Dax shook his head and took another step forward.

"Jane, this is my sister; my twin sister."

"Dalila." She smiled from behind Dax, waving shyly. I blinked between the two of them, just now recognizing the similarities.

"Oh, wow." I breathed out, feeling stupidly embarrassed. "I'm Jane."

"Jane." Dalila looked at Dax and then back to me. "I've heard about you." My cheeks flushed as she looked over me. "You were right Dax, she's gorgeous." Dax scratched the back of his head and smiled softly.

"Dalila... prefers women." He chuckled as she craned her neck to the side, looking at my butt.

"And if my brother weren't so smitten with you, love, I'd take you-"

"That's enough, Dal!" Dax yelled, grabbing his sister by the wrist and pulling her toward his house.

"I would like to invite you over for dinner this evening! Let's say seven?" She winked as Dax successfully pulled her through his front door. Trying to suppress my smile, I bit my lip and walked inside my house, throwing my bag on the bed.

"Viv, I have dinner plans tonight!"

At six-thirty, Viv and I looked at ourselves in the mirror. She looked gorgeous in her soft pink mini dress and curled, fire red hair. She styled me in a red wine colored dress that came up mid-thigh and a pair of beat up, black converse - which we had to compromise on - instead of the six inch heels she threw to me in the beginning. I had to admit though, I looked good; more than good, I looked awesome.

"I had no idea that when I've been invited somewhere, it meant both of us will be in attendance." I jabbed her ribs lightly with my elbow, a bright smile resonating on my face.

"Oh shut up," She rolled her eyes and giggled, "Just admit you're excited to see Dax."

"I just miss my friend." I shrugged, walking out of her bedroom as I slipped a pair of pearl earrings on. Viv rolled her eyes again.

"Please," She scoffed. "You couldn't want each other more unless you both had magnets in your pants." I gasped and swatted her arm, which only caused her to laugh. "I wished you'd just break it off with Riley already and get with the guy you actually want. I don't understand what's stopping you."

"Riley is who I should be with." I sighed, handing her the house keys.

"But you want Dax. No, you need Dax." She shook me softly. "Open your eyes." I bit my lip, looking at the clock for an escape.

"We're going to be late." I grabbed her wrist and pulled her out the door. It was one of those rare cold nights in California, I thought about going in to grab a jacket up opted against it. The door swung open before we had the chance to knock, Dalila standing in the doorway to greet us.

"Hola, hola, hola!" She squealed, pulling me into a tight hug. "And who do we have here?" She sidestepped me to get to Vivian, a sheepish smile now plastered on my best friends mouth. Shy and Vivian rarely ever mixed. Vivian's freckled cheeks were bright red as Dax's sister approached her.

"This is my best friend, Vivian." I said, unsure if Dalila had even heard me, being that she was so intoxicated by the sight of the woman in front of her.

"Vivian." The name fell from Dalila's lips the way mine had from Dax's. And for some reason, I knew Vivian was a goner. Vivian swallowed, hard.

"Let's all come inside, dinner is ready." Dax appeared at the door and I smiled softly, hoping that tonight would help the tension in our relationship. Dalila escorted Vivian inside, leaving Dax and me to ourselves.

"Weird to think I've never been inside your house." I said, glancing at him from the side. A smirk lifted on his lips slightly as he nodded.

"The only view you've had is from your bedroom." He joked and for a moment, I felt like nothing had changed between us. I yearned to hug him, but I refrained. "I guess we should go in-side before my sister devours Vivian." I chuckled and followed behind him. The entrance of Dax's home was extravagant. The walls were made up of dark paneled wood, littered with frames of art. As we entered the dining room, I took in the sight of a crystal chandelier that hung from the middle of the ceiling;

just below was a long mahogany table set with four chairs face across from each other. Vivian and Dalila were already sitting across from each other, in the middle of hushed, deep conversation.

"Dalila." Dax call as he walked to the kitchen. His sister didn't even look up as she whispered things to my best friend, who was giggling like a little school girl. "Dalila." He called again, a little louder. Again, the women stayed infatuated by each other. "Dalila Maria Guadalupe Rivera!" He yelled and Dalila sprang up, hustling to the kitchen.

"Wow." I mouthed, sitting adjacent to Vivian. "What have you two been talking about?" Vivian blushed and shook her head just before the two siblings reemerged with dishes of food. In one pan was cut up steak; a stone mortar held crushed avocado, tomato, and cilantro; a covered bowl held warm tortillas, and two ceramic bowls were filled to the brim with fried rice and re-fried black beans.

"Oh my." Vivian said, taking in the glory of the meal in front of us.

"Let's eat, yeah?" Dax smiled, grabbing my plate from in front of me and placing three pieces of the steak on my plate as well as a generous spoonful of each of the side dishes. Saying a silent thank you, my mouth began to water with hunger, but I waited until everyone had been plated before I dug in. Dax glanced at me from across the table, a smirk on his face as I stuffed mine. Realizing I was being watched, I swallowed the contents of my mouth and felt my cheeks flush with embarrassment.

"It's delicious, thank you both so much." Vivian smiled, crossing her fork and knife over her plate.

"Yeah." Dax scoffed. "Dalila can't cook."

"You made this?" I cocked an eyebrow in surprise. Dax feigned offense, placing his hand against his chest in mock hurt.

"Do I not look the type to be a Master Chef?" He questioned, a coy smile on his face.

"I just assumed you were the type to want a woman in your kitchen." I rebutted, crossing my arms over my chest. Dax stood and grabbed my plate from me, adding more food.

"I'm a big boy, I can cook and clean for myself. Why should it be the responsibility of the woman I love to care for me like I am a child?" He handed the plate back to me and picked up his own, walking back to the kitchen. When I turned to talk to Vivian, I realized both she and Dalila were gone. Suddenly alone, I watched as Dax came in and stopped abruptly.

"Where's Vivian and my sister?" His eyes were trained on me and I immediately felt squeamish.

"Gone?" I suggested with a halfhearted shrug. Dax rolled his eyes, smirking slightly.

"Really?" He remarked sarcastically, "Viv probably already has her dress ripped off."

"Oh?" I said, feeling at ease with Dax's playful side emerging. He shrugged and took a drink from his scotch glass, sitting down across from me once again. Silence enveloped us. Minutes went by, maybe seconds but it was hard to tell. I wished for our old relationship back, but it seemed hardly attainable.

"So-" We managed to interrupted each other with the same word.

"How've you been?" I bit my lip, trying to conceal my nerves.

"Good." He replied, his finger drifting across the rim of his glass. "You?"

"Good." I said quickly, nodding. "Your sister is lovely."

"Yeah," He chuckled. "Lovely." Silence. I wanted so badly to reach for him, the words I couldn't say brought to life by action. But I went against my judgement and stayed still.

"I miss you." I mumbled, looking out the circular window that looked over his backyard. Dax was quiet for a long time.

"I miss you, too." My heart warmed at the thought. "You look... great." After all the times I had pushed him away, he was holding back now, I could feel it. Without allowing myself to think, I stood and walked over to his chair, tugging on his large arm. He silently stood, watching me closely as I wrapped my arms around him. He didn't move and for a fleeting moment I was overwhelmed by embarrassment, and debated on running away, selling the house, and moving several states away. But his arms slowly encased around me and his warmth surrounded my body. For the first time in over a week, I felt safe.

"Dax! Jane!" Vivian and Dalila called from the hallway, running toward the dining room. Dax and I quickly pulled away from each other, just as the two girls appeared.

"We're going clubbing, join us." Dalila said, catching Vivian's chin between her thumb and index finger in a sweet gesture.

"Okay." Dax shrugged, grabbing his keys from the counter. I shook my head.

"Count me out." Viv frowned at me, grabbing me by the shoulders and pushing me toward the door.

"You're coming, it doesn't matter what you say." She continued to push.

"Dax, you're a cop, you can stop this!" I called out to him for help. He smirked, following behind my best friend and his sister.

"You said yourself you've never been to a club. Tonight seems to be full of unexpected things, I suppose clubbing will be added to that list." And before I knew it, I was in the back seat of Dax's muscle car, on the way to go clubbing for the first time with my best friend, a cop, and his sister.

11

CHAPTER 11

"No." I shook my head, looking up at the vibrating walls of the Echo. Vivian patted my butt gently to usher me forward.

"You don't have an option," She feigned a regretful frown before slipping into line with Dalila. "You're going to love it, I promise!" I sauntered in line behind them with Dax following suit. As the two women in front of us flirted and giggled with each other, Dax and I stood awkwardly silent. After being interrupted in the middle of an intimate hug that I had initiated, I wasn't sure how to start a conversation again. So we just didn't talk. By the time we entered the bursting building, the place had become packed with sweaty, intoxicated people. Between the bar and the dance floor, people drunkenly dance against each other in an alcohol-fueled sexual desire.

"What's your drink, Pequeño?" Dalila called over the music. I shook my head, knowing that if I could control anything in this situation, it'd be my sobriety. Dalila pulled her brother up to the bar and disappeared to retrieve drinks for everyone. When the siblings returned, they brought two trays with four small glasses on each.

"I've got shots!"Dalila beamed, setting her tray on the table we had found. Each of them grabbed a glass while I watched with growing nervousness, my stomach knotting as my eyes gazed over each of their waiting faces.

"You want me to drink?" I bit my lip as I looked at the liquid. Dax looked away quickly, throwing back his shot.

"Just take these two shots, for me," Vivian pleaded. "Let loose for once!" Releasing my lip from my teeth, I nodded hesitantly.

"I, 2, 3!" We all threw our heads back, my throat burning harshly from the alcohol.

"What is this?" I choked out as they handed me the second one.

"Tequila."

Two, three, four, five, six shots later. My stomach warmed with the help of my best friend Tequila. Dalila and Vivian eloped to the dance floor where they flirtatiously danced and touched each other. I sat on a cushioned bar stool, eating olives and Maraschino cherries. Dax had disappeared long ago, leaving me to my drunken thoughts. A hand appeared on my thigh and I whirled around in hope to see my favorite cop.

"Hey," A tall man with a five o' clock shadow slurred down at me. A gold chain around his neck dangled over his white wife beat which made me giggle with the thought of Jersey Shore. "Can I get you a drink?

"Tequi-"

"No, she's good." A voice growled from behind the tall man. I craned my neck around to see Dax's angry expression, his arms folded across his chest in a protective father-like manner. The tall man scoffed and turned back to me, leaning against the bar to appear nonchalant.

"So what's your name, Sweetheart?" He purred to me, his finger gripping harder on my thigh. "How about that drink?" As I fumbled with something to say, fingers gripped the back of the tall man's neck and pulled him backward, his fingernails scratching my thigh as they left my skin. Dax filled the void of the tall stranger, looking down at me disapprovingly.

"What were you doing talking to him?" He scowled, ordering himself his signature scotch, neat.

"Um," I couldn't find words.

"He was going to drug you, you know." Dax jaw flexed under the skin of his cheek as he held up a small bag of pills. "Pick-pocketed these from him when he was walking over to you." I cocked an eyebrow at him.

"You knew he was going to target me?" I looked between the bag and Dax. He rolled his eyes, annoyed by the conversation before the bartender slid his drink across the table. Dax downed the liquid with ease.

"Please, you know you're the most beautiful girl here. If it weren't him, it'd be any other guy. I've been picking them away from you all night." He groaned. A smirk threatened my lips as my stomach exploded with butterflies.

"You've been shielding me from guys all night?" I crossed my legs. Dax paled slightly, knowing he was boxed in.

"Well-"

"Why would you do that?" I interjected, not being able to control the ridiculous smile plastered on my face.

"It's my job." He answered unconvincingly, staring down at his empty glass. Deciding to let him off, I nodded and ordered myself another shot. "Are you sure you can handle another? You're pretty wasted already."

"I'm fine." I nodded, swallowing a burp that was trying to escape my throat. Scanning the crowd for Vivian and Dalila, my eyes settled on a surprisingly sight.

"Riley?" I whispered, watching as he sloppily stuck his tongue down the throat of a skinny blonde on the dance floor. The bartender returned with my shot and I threw it back to distract my thoughts. Feeling the liquid courage course through me, I hopped off the stool and stalked forward. Once my boyfriend and his date were directly in front of me, I tapped him on the shoulder. "Hey, babe." I mocked his pet name for me. Riley turned and choked on air.

"Jane."

"Who's this?" The blonde sputtered drunkenly, her red lipstick smeared across her mouth. I shook my head in disgust.

"What are you doing here?" Riley let go of the blonde to grab my arms.

"I could ask the same thing." I shrugged, feeling surprisingly numb to the situation.

"This- She-" Riley's eyes were suddenly looking past me. "Of course you're here." I turned, watching Riley glare at Dax. "You know what, Jane? Go ahead and fuck around with your loser cop." He pushed me into Dax's awaiting chest, his warm hands catching me before I could fall. "Brittney isn't even the first girl I've been with tonight." Riley winked before locking lips with the blonde once again. Dax made sure I was standing upright before charging forward.

"Push her again, I dare you-" I quickly grabbed Dax's arm before he did anything he would regret tomorrow, pulling him back toward the bar. "Stop it, Jane!" He yelled, yanking his hand from my grip. I stood silently, looking at my converse-clad feet. Dax sighed and shook his head. "I need some air." Before I could object, Dax stalked out the door.

"Jane!" Vivian grabbed me forcefully. "Jane, are you okay? We just saw Riley-"

"I'm fine." I nodded reassuringly, forcing a smile. Vivian pulled me in to a tight embrace anyway.

"Jane, why don't you come out and dance with us? Dancing is a constructive way to deal with emotion." Dalila suggested, her hand squeezing my shoulder comfortingly.

"I don't know..." I bit my lip, feeling a mess of thoughts and feelings that needed to be sorted out.

"C'mon, Jay. You're a great dancer." Vivian moved a few strands of hair away from my eyes and smiled softly. "It'll be fun, and if it's not, just say the word and we can leave." I looked between Dalila and my best friend.

"Okay." I shrugged halfheartedly, allowing them to pull me on the florescent-lit dance floor. The two of them melted into one as they danced closely to each other. The heavy, upbeat rhythm of the music began to move me, the alcohol giving me the extra push I needed.

"That's it, love." Dalila grinned over at me as my arms shot up in the air and my hips swayed with the music. One song dissolved into another, the changing from upbeat to slow and sensual. The crowd enveloped me, Dalila and Vivian lost in their own bubble of infatuation to notice me anymore. As my hips made a move backward, a large pair of hands gripped them from behind with gentle force. His cologne wrapped around me in erotic familiarity as he leaned in the exposed flesh of my neck.

"I'm sorry for walking out, I just needed to calm down." He whispered against me, his lips grazing against my skin. A fleet of goosebumps appeared and I pressed myself further against him.

"But you're here now." I mumbled in response, running my fingers over his hands that still held my hips. He leaned in, his lips now against my ear as one of his hands trailed down the length of my thigh.

"Dance with me." He said, pressing my backside against his pelvis and guiding my hips with his to move to the slow beat of the song. My heart hammered in my chest, but my body was completely at ease with Dax's presence. Without thinking, my arms weaved around to tangle in his hair, something that Dax greatly approved of as he pulled me impossibly closer. I could feel the hard muscles of his chest against my back as his head dipped into the crook of my neck. Sweat began to slick our skin as we mirrored each other's movements, our hands not able to touch, pull, or feel enough. Dax suddenly spun me around to face him, our heavy breathing now mixing in the small space between our lips. His fingers dug into the fabric of the dress that covered my hips and I moaned ever so softly. And if the song hadn't ended just as the sound had left my lips, Dax maybe wouldn't have even heard it. But that wasn't the case.

His eyes clouded over, darkening with something I had never seen in him before. I gasped softly, my stomach knotting once again as his pupils dilated at the sight of my lips so close to his.

"Tell me you want it." He pressed his sweaty forehead against mine. "Say it."

"I-I," I couldn't speak, the sheer amount of desire, lust, and alcohol clouded my mind indefinitely. His darkened green eyes peered into mine, stripping me of all thoughts that were beyond him. "I want it. Kiss me." I cried out softly. And without another beat, his lips pressed against mine. Explosions erupted in my brain, waves of heat flowing between my legs. My fingers fisted his hair as the kiss deepened, my lips parting with another sound of pleasure. His experienced lips moved against mine in a hungry, yet gentle manner while his hands gripped me as if I would disappear at any moment.

And suddenly, he stopped. I watched him in shock as he regained himself, his eyes turning back to the bright green I was used to.

"Not like this." He shook his head, holding his hand out to me. "I want you sober, so that you can remember everything I do to you and how it feels." He sighed, brushing his thumb across my disappointed lips. "You will agree with me tomorrow, when you're not drunk." He wrapped his arm around my waist and signaled to Dalila and Vivian. I was walked out of the club and lifted into the car where I fell asleep. My eyes lazily drifted open momentarily as Dax slipped me into my bed and cover me up with blankets.

"Thank you." Vivian said from the doorway.

"It's not a problem." Dax responded, kissing my forehead.

"Seriously though, thank you. She's happy." Viv paused. "I missed seeing her smile. When she's around you, she's like the old her." I slipped back into unconsciousness before I could listen to the rest of their conversation.

12

CHAPTER 12

The next morning was filled with undeniable pain. My brain felt like it may bust from my skull with every movement. My eyes were shaded by sunglasses to escape the beams of light that shone through the curtains while I puked my guts out in the toilet. Vivian rubbed my back soothingly before helping me back to bed. When the covers were pulled up to my chin, a waste basket by my side in case of any more sporadic vomiting, and a few Aspirin to choke down with a glass of water, Vivian left me to sleep.

Hours drifted by with me coming in and out of consciousness. When my door opened and closed, my sleepy eyes gazed at the LED lit alarm clock that read: 3:00 PM. I had slept all day, something I never do.

"Princesa." He called from behind me, to which I slowly turned on my side to view Dax with a bottle of Sprite. "My mother claims that Sprite helps settle the stomach."

"I'll keep that in mind." I smile slightly and accept the bottle. As I twisted the cap, the carbonized air burst from the opening, small bubbles coming to the surface with a soft fizz. I took a small sip and then another, and another. The liquid soon consumed my stomach instead of the bottle, which Dax gently removed from my hands and threw away.

"How are you feeling?" He asked, lounging in the desk chair he had pulled up to my bed. I shrugged, unable to give an accurate verbal representation of nausea and migraines without sounding disgusting. "Well, I was just coming by to see if you were okay."

"I am." I swallowed the bile that rose to my throat to prove myself truthful.

"But as the lead on your parent's case, I have to inform you, there's been a string of murders within a ten mile radius of Ophelia Avenue. We don't know if it correlates with Dorian Smith, but it's oddly coincidental." I felt sick again, my stomach churning with a mixture of my hangover and Dax's news. I whipped the blankets away from my feet and sprinted for the bathroom. Falling to my knees, I cradled the toilet and emptied the content of my stomach. I felt Dax's hands move the hair away from my neck, wrapping it around his knuckles to hold it back from my spewing mouth. Exhausted, I rolled and slumped against the cold porcelain bathtub. "I'm sorry." He said softly, watching me closely.

"It's not your fault Dax." I tried to smile reassuringly, but came up short. After a long silence between us, Dax slipped his hands around my waist and pulled me to my feet.

"I'm going to draw you a bath," He pulled the lid over the toilet and sat me down. "Warm water settles a troubled stomach and a troubled mind."

"Dax-"

"Shh," He murmured, placing his index finger against my lips. "Trust me." And I did. I let him fill the tub with steaming water while I retreated to the seclusion of my bedroom to undress. Once my robe was secured around me, I reentered the bathroom to see mounds of bubbles all across the surface of the water and Dax lighting a candle he had found in the closet.

"Wow," I mumbled, biting my lip. My toes met the soft fabric of the rug and I felt the steam against my thighs. "Thank you." He silently pulled me closer and brushed his fingers across plush material of the robe.

"I remember the first time I saw you in this." He muttered. For a moment, I couldn't remember ever wearing my robe in front of Dax, but then I realized how we had been introduced. My cheeks burned with embarrassment at the memory and Dax chuckled quietly. We stood there a long time, just him holding me. I took a step back, realizing the lines between us were becoming muddled into something else, something I couldn't handle right now.

"Well, I guess I'd better get in before the water gets cold." I laughed awkwardly, but he didn't move. "Uh, Dax?"

"Yeah?"

"Aren't you going to step outside?" I questioned.

"No, why?" He asked quizzically.

"Oh, maybe because I'll be naked?" I cocked an eyebrow. Dax rolled his eyes and leaned against the sink.

"Oh, please, Princesa." He chuckled softly. "I've seen you naked before, why are you so bashful suddenly? Should I turn on some MC Hammer?" I poked his chest.

"Not funny." I frowned. He laughed and shook his head fondly.

"Fine, I'll shut my eyes." He cover his eyes with his hands and I watched him in disbelief.

"I'm not undressing in front of you!" I hissed playfully, crossing my arms over my chest.

"Well, I'm not leaving. You're still hung over and Vivan left for work, I'm the only one who could get you to the hospital if your clumsy ass gets hurt somehow."

"How would I get hurt in the bathtub?" I scrunched up my nose stubbornly.

"You would find a way." Dax smiled cockily.

"I'm not undressing in front of you-"

"Three..." He began to count.

"I'm not playing around, Dax."

"Neither am I, now get your ass in the tub; two..."

"No-"

"One..." When Dax was about to move his hands away from his eyes, I squealed and pulled off the robe, jumping into the hot water as fast as I could. Hitting my elbow on the tiling of the wall, I scowled in pain. "Ha. Told you." He winked. I rolled my eyes and settled into the warm abyss. A ding sounded from the sink and I looked at Dax questioningly. He placed my phone in my hand.

"It's been going off for awhile," He sighed, scratching the back of his head. "It's Riley."

"Oh." I mumbled, scrolling through the messages. "I wonder what he's apologizing for." Dax's brow furrowed quickly, his lips pursing into a thin line.

"You don't remember last night?" He whispered softly, but I could feel the air become tense.

"No..." I shook my head, cursing myself for being so negligent. "What happened?"

"I think it should come from him." Dax's jaw flexed under his skin and he turned away from me. "I better go." He stood and reached for the door.

"Please, don't go." I begged, avoiding his eyes as he looked back at me. With a sigh, he sat on the toilet lid and looked at the floor. I didn't know what happened last night, or why he was so upset over Riley. But one thing I did know was, I didn't want to be anywhere but by Dax's side.

13

CHAPTER 13

The next day, I was back to normal. The migraines faded and the nausea left, leaving me to clean up the mess in my social life. Dax was upset about something that happened that night at the club, and Riley was blowing up my phone with apologetic messages and voicemails. I wished I could remember what had happened, so I knew how to feel and how assess each situation.

So when I finally felt well enough to answer Riley's call, I found myself back at his parent's restaurant. When I arrived, a waiter seated me at a table in the back, where I was told to wait for Riley. Ten minutes had passed before Riley appeared from the kitchen, holding two plates of food and a bottle of wine. He set the plate down and poured me a glass of the aged Chardonnay, but said nothing.

"What happened at the club?" I finally broke the silence, Riley's face paling slightly at my question. He cleared his throat.

"I was drunk- Upset and drunk." He said, glancing up at me and then back down to his food.

"Upset about what?" I pressed, watching as he squirmed in his seat. His normally warm eyes seemed guarded, defensive even.

"You." He replied, taking a large gulp from his glass.

"Me?" I found myself pointing to myself in confusion.

"We've been dating for a couple months, I was getting tired of waiting." He avoided my confused stare, "When you turned me down, I was really hurt. I kept thinking there was something wrong with me, maybe you thought I wasn't attractive enough, I don't know."

"Riley-"

"Let me finish." He bit his lip before continuing, "My friends asked me if I wanted to go out, and I stupidly agreed. I was just so bummed out, Jane. You have no idea how awful I felt about myself. Anyway, we get to the club and we drink. A lot. Before I know it, I'm plastered and fucking four girls in the bathroom." I choke on air, noticing a few heads in the restaurant turn toward us. Pushing my embarrassment aside, I watch him in disbelief. "And then I see you there with him, and I just freaked out. I shouldn't have pushed you." He dipped his head down dejectedly. "I'm sorry." I was quiet, minutes passed and I had said nothing.

"Please say something." He pulled my hands into his. Their familiarity seemed distant now.

"I forgive you." I sighed, removing one of my hands from his to gently squeeze his arm comfortingly. He let out a deep sigh of relief and leaned forward to kiss me. But I, of course, pulled away. "Right, you need time." Riley nodded stiffly, but I shook my head.

"No, I forgive you, but we're done." And for the first time since my parents died, I felt strong. I backed out of my chair and stood, leaving Riley at his overrated, overly expensive table to dine alone. Once I reached the parking lot, I opened my car door and was about to get in when I saw Riley exit the building.

"You can't leave me! I settled for you, I could've had any girl I wanted but I chose you!" He came up to my car and slammed the door, cornering me between himself and the vehicle. "You don't leave me, I leave you."

"Fine." I shrug, craning my neck to the side to avoid his heavy breathing.

"Do you not give a shit at all?" Riley spat, desperately trying to rouse me in some way. Part of me was sad about losing my relationship with Riley, I felt like I had wasted so much time with the wrong guy. When I didn't say anything, Riley pushed himself away from my car and turned away from me. After a few moments, he whirled back around to face me, pointing his index finger toward me. "This is because of Dax, isn't it?"

"Yes." I said without another heartbeat. His skin paled slightly and he shook his head.

"I should've known," He chuckled maniacally and grabbed my chin roughly. "Have fun with your nobody cop, slut." Riley shoved my face away and he walked back into the restaurant.

My heart pounded hard in my chest, but not because Riley had hurt me. My heart was pounding because I was free. I jumped into my car and pulled out of the parking spot, speeding onto the highway.

Half an hour later, I found myself at Dax's door. With the sudden adrenaline I had an endless supply of today, I knocked at the door continuously. But after minutes of knocking, I realized he wasn't home. I dejectedly walked home, my feet dragging against the sidewalk. As I approached my front door, I ran my fingers through my hair and sighed.

"What would you have said to him?" I asked myself, my forehead against the cool wooden door. "I'm single now, let's finally makeout?" Scoffing at myself, I shoved the key into the lock and opened the door, shutting it flatly behind me. I threw my purse on the couch and made my way to my bedroom before seeing the door was already open. On guard, I quietly tiptoed inside. The bedroom was empty and I let out a sigh of relief.

"Dal, just make sure everything's ready. I'm waiting for her to get home right no-" Our eyes met as he exited my bathroom, a duffel bag in hand with a variety of my stuff inside. "I'll... Call you back." He hung up, but we continued to stare at each other. "I can explain this."

"Please do." I nodded breathlessly.

"After you left this morning, Dorian Smith broke into your house and took Vivian hostage," My heart sunk, black spots appearing in my vision. "Thank God Dalila was coming over to take Viv out. Dal shot Dorian in the thigh, giving her enough time to get Vivian out safely, but Dorian got away." My heart lifted slightly at the thought of Vivian being safe. "But he knows where you live now, you can't stay here. We're leaving."

"Leaving where?" I bit my lip as he continued to pack my bag.

"Mexico."

14

—— ◆ ——

CHAPTER 14

I didn't get a chance to be on my phone until we were driving down the highway. Traffic was awful and despite it being December, it was still in the high eighties. I peeled out of my light jacket that I had thrown on just as Vivian answered her phone.

"Jane?" She called into the receiver shakily. Tears welled in my eyes as I smiled at the sound of her voice.

"Hey Viv, are you okay?" I let my head hang down in sorrow, "I'm sorry to get you mixed up in all of this."

"Stop it right now, you're my best friend, Jay. Don't you think for one second that I'd want to be anywhere else but in mortal danger with you." We laughed, I missed her. "So where are you?"

"On my way to Mexico," I laughed in disbelief, "With Dax... Where are you?"

"Miami, as soon as Dalila rescued me, she booked us a flight to her house down here. It's gorgeous, Jane. I wish you could be here." Vivian gushed and I smiled out of happiness for her.

"Well, we might not be seeing you too soon, Dax didn't want to take a plane because flights are easily traceable. We're driving."

"Isn't that like, a twenty-seven hour drive?" Vivian asked and I nodded to myself.

"Yeah, and it doesn't help there's a ton of traffic." I chimed sarcastically, glancing at Dax from the corner of my eye. His jaw was clenched in irritation, we'd moved very little in the hour we'd been on the highway.

"Jeez, well, let me send you this playlist. It'll take your mind off of the time." My phone chirped with a notification and my eyebrows cocked in confusion.

"Thanks, Viv, but I better go. Looks like the cars in front of us are moving a bit faster."

"Okay, just call me when you get to Mexico, alright? Maybe we could Skype." She suggested, making me smile.

"Sounds like a plan. Love you, Viv." I made a kiss sound with my lips.

"Love you, Jay." She cooed in return before we hung up the phone. I reclined in Dax's passenger seat, the black fabric feeling hot and uncomfortable. Dax's mood seemed to lift as we exited off the main highway and turned onto the interstate, the GPS making it known that we would be on this road for a hundred or so miles.

"Do you mind if I play so music?" I asked quietly, suddenly feeling like a little mouse. An hour and a half ago, I was ready to proclaim my feelings for him. Now I felt like I might melt into a puddle if he even looked in my direction.

"That'd be great. Maybe I could relax a tad." He chuckled softly, but his voice sounded tight and hoarse. I nodded and plug the aux cord into my phone, selected the playlist Vivian had sent me. As I scrolled through the list, I realized I'd never heard any of these songs. The first came on, a heavy slow song that made me want to move like I was exotic dancer.

Hold me close I'm wasting away / Hold me close I'm too fucked to stand

I gasped quietly as the beginning lyrics sounded through the speaker system. From the corner of my eye, I watched Dax's eyebrows shoot up. If I survive this, I'm going to kill Vivian. But to play it cool, I let the song continue to play.

Clothes in front of your new daddy / Stick my ass out for all it's worth / Stay like this until the grave daddy / Drop your ass, what's your self esteem worth?

"This is Vivian's playlist," I bit my lip and he glanced over at me, his eyes drifting to my mouth.

"I figured." He licked his bottom lip and I felt my teeth bite down harder on my own. Something had changed within the car, something about the air. It was thicker, hotter than moments ago but when I peeked at the temperature gauge, the heat hadn't shifted. Beads of sweat cascaded down my neck, following the curve of my throat and slipped down my cleavage. I needed to take something else off to cool down, but I knew it may stir trouble. But after several minutes of near heatstroke, I tore off my tee shirt and threw it into the back seat, leaving me in my white cropped tank top.

After a few more songs, it was hard to think about anything but my sexual frustration. I wanted to jump into the driver's seat and straddle the man, but the logical and sensible part of me knew that was dangerous for more reasons than one. When the seventh song came on, I had to put it to a stop. I reached for my phone to switch to a less sexual ensemble, but Dax's hand met mine.

"I like this song, do you mind if we listen to it all the way through?" He glanced at me, something in his eyes made nod and listen. His lips moved to the lyrics of the song, his tongue lulling each word like a quiet symphony. Oh lord, please help me. "Like a cop I'm cuffing I'm copping a feel / Little mama got ass when she walk in them heels / She love when I eat it, she make it meal / Baby girl, screaming / I give her the pillow so no one can hear." He sang softly and as if he spoke the magic words, my underwear became saturated.

"Oh lord, give me strength," I mumbled, swallowing hard. "How many more hours?"

"Twenty-three, but if you wanted to stop at a hotel, we can." Dax offered as he lifted his shirt over his head, flinging it in the backseat like I had. My mouth ran dry and I quickly looked out of the window. Count the trees, clouds, and birds.

"No, let's just keep going." I ran my fingers through my hair. This was going to be a long drive.

15

— ◦ —

CHAPTER 15

Dax had been up all night driving, so when he began to swerve along the road, I made him switch to the passenger seat. Moving the seat up, I situated the rear view mirror to my eye level and pressed on the gas. Dax quickly fell asleep, night turned into morning. With only thirteen hours to go and without the distraction of Dax, I found the drive incredibly peaceful. The lush green landscape that occupied cows and deer slowly turned into dessert, filled with cacti and tumbleweed, snakes and roadrunners. It was hard to believe that climate and scenery could change so drastically in one country. After another few hours, Dax reawakened and yawned, stretching his long tattooed limbs.

"How close are we?" He asked hoarsely, running his fingers over his face to wipe away the sleep.

"About nine hours." I replied simply, nodding my head along to a song I had found when flipping through radio stations. He was quiet for a long time, I thought he had even fallen asleep.

"How'd your talk with Riley go?" He finally spoke up and I felt a sudden burst of shyness.

"Good, I suppose." I bit my lip, keeping my eyes on the road.

"He told you what he did?" He pressed, his voice sounding strained.

"Yes," I nodded, "And I broke up with him."

"Oh," Dax mumbled, "I'm sorry."

"It needed to happen." I gnawed at my lip, find the right words. There it was again, the shift in the air. Something hot and dense, like I was going to burst. When the gas light flickered on, I eagerly exited the interstate to get to a gas station. I need a drink. With Dax pumping gas into his car, I shuffled into the dingy gas station, the air conditioning wafting me like a glorious antarctic breeze. The cashier sent me a hello and I made my way to the refrigerator section. Sprite, Fanta, Mountain Dew, Coke, Pepsi; there's too many to choose from. I opted for the Pepsi and made my up to the counter, just as Dax walked in. In the bright light of the afternoon sun, I was able to get a full view of his tattoos, each one looking beautiful on his skin. I wanted to get to know each of them.

"Gas and the soda." Dax said, nodding toward me with the bottle in my hand. The cashier nodded and typed our items into the register.

"You kids on a road trip?" The cashier questioned while Dax handed him the money.

"Something like that." Dax chuckled, collecting his change and shoving it into his back pocket.

"You don't mind all those tattoos?" The cashier craned his neck around Dax to look at me. My cheeks heated and I shook my head.

"No, I like them." I mumbled, letting my hair fall in front of my face to hide my coyness. Dax's lips quirked slightly into a smirk.

"You two are a sweet couple, have fun on your trip." The cashier smiled and for some reason, neither Dax nor I corrected the man. We walked out to Dax's car in silence, me holding my soda and him holding his keys. I slipped into the passenger seat and leaned into it, closing my eyes and trying not to smile. Dax seemed silently happy too, so I didn't say anything. I didn't want this moment of bliss to pass.

We arrived in a small town called San Sebastian Bernal. The streets were made of cobblestone and the buildings were old and beautiful. Near the outskirts, Dax pulled into the driveway of a large pueblo home made of earth and clay, etched with designs and painted with vibrant colors of yellow and turquoise. Dax collected our bags from the trunk and I followed him up the pathway that led up to the home. When we were a couple feet away from the door, several people poured out of the front door.

"Mi hijo, mi hijo!" An older woman threw her hands around Dax's middle, pulling him close. I smiled at the interaction between them, Dax embracing her warmly. "Mi hijo está en casa!" A younger woman followed close behind, her hair jet black and her skin glowingly sun kissed.

"Bienvenido a casa, hermano." She said, joining in on the hug. Everyone stopped at the sound of a little girl's laugh and Dax bent down just in time to catch her in his arms.

"Oh, mi hermosa sobrina!" He cooed to her, kissing her cheeks repeatedly. I stood awkwardly in the background, watching their sweet homecoming like it was a movie.

"Daxon, ¿quién es?" All four of them looked back at me, Dax's mouth picking up in a slight smirk as I blushed.

"Todos, esta es Jane." I waved at Dax's introduction, gingerly flicking some hair out of my face.

"Es maravilloso conocerte, querida-" The older woman began to say before Dax stopped her.

"No, no mamá, Jane no habla español." The two women looked between each other before giving their attention back to me.

"It is... Very nice to meet you, Jane." The younger woman prompted, holding out her hand to me, "My name is Darcy, I am Daxon's sister and this is my daughter Emilia." She lifted the toddler into her arms. The beautiful little girl smile brightly, black curls covering the top of her head. I couldn't help but smile back at the dimpled child.

"Hello, Darcy," I waved at the toddler, "Hello, Emilia." A small hand reached out and touched my cheek.

"Hola." Emilia giggled, squeezing my cheek gently before squirming out of her mother's grip and running inside the house. The older woman stepped in and pulled me in to a tight embrace, her small figure stronger than I had expected.

"Hello, Jane, I have heard very much about you." She said as she pulled away. "Come inside, you must be exhausted." The two women hurried inside, leaving Dax and me standing in the pathway.

"You brought me to your family's home?" I cocked an eyebrow at him.

"It's the only place I trust." He shrugged and picked up the bags once more, nodding toward the door. "C'mon." I followed him inside and he showed me to the guest bedroom. The bed itself was a twin sized mattress covered in a homemade quilt, a handcrafted dresser was flush against the wall with a mirror on top. A beautiful mural of the sun was painted on the ceiling in bright oranges, yellows, and reds.

"It's lovely, thank you." I said, unpacking some of my things into the dresser. Dax stood in the door for a moment, watching me. "What?"

"I don't know," He chuckled, playing with his fingers. "I guess I just never thought I'd see you standing in my childhood home." Unsure of how to respond, I sat on the bed and watched the floor. "I realized I forgot to pack you something to sleep in so," He pulled his grey short sleeved tee off and handed it to me, "I'll leave you to unpack." Standing stunned for a moment, I shook my head to gain reality and grabbed the landline phone, dialing Vivian's number.

"Hello?" She answered.

"Hey Viv, just wanted to let you know you're on my shit list." I hissed, closing the guest room door.

"Little old me?" Vivian cried innocently, "Why's that?"

"Maybe because I spent the first have of the drive to Mexico listening to your sex playlist with Dax" I growled lowly, falling backwards into the bed.

"I know!" She squealed happily. "Did anything happen between you two?"

"No! Was that your plan?" I whisper-yelled, trying to control my hysteria.

"Obviously! We want you and Dax to get together already. It's borderline annoying that you haven't." She said, pushing blame onto me.

"I know." I sighed exhaustively, wiping sweat away from my forehead.

"Wait, you agree with me?" Vivian sang in disbelief.

"Yes," I laughed, missing my best friend. "But I should get going. I don't want to rack up a huge long distance call bill for Dax's mother."

"You're at his family home? Oh my gosh, Jane, something is going to happen between you two, I know it." I rolled my eyes and shook my head, my cheeks beginning to ache from my smile.

"I really have to go, Viv. Love you."

"Love you."

16

CHAPTER 16

I stirred in the middle of the night, flipping from one side of the bed to the other. After almost an hour of tossing and turning, I slipped on my robe and tiptoed into the kitchen. With intent of thanking Dax's mother in the morning, I went into the fridge and pulled out a pitcher of milk, pouring myself half a glass and throwing it in the microwave to warm up. The timer beeped a few times before I took it out. I leaned against the stone counter tops and sipped at the warm milk, humming softly in comfort.

"Fancy meeting you here." A deep voice whispered from the door frame. Nearly dropping the glass, I steadied myself and attempted to look nonchalant. Dax walked into the kitchen, sporting simply a pair of basketball shorts. And nothing else. His hair disheveled by sleep and his voice hoarse from exhaustion.

"Yeah, I couldn't sleep." I looked down at the glass and nervously held it toward him, "Milk?" Dax chuckled lowly and shook his head.

"No thanks, Princesa." He stepped toward me, but I was stupidly frozen to the floor so he had to maneuver around me. He pulled out a chunk of chocolate and grabbed my glass of milk, pouring it down the sink. Dax lit a flame on the stove and simmered the chocolate in a saucepan of milk. After a few minutes, he sprinkled a mixture of cinnamon and sugar into it and added a shot of vanilla before stirring the brew. He poured both of us a mug full and after it had cooled, I took a sip.

"Oh my gosh, this is amazing." I moaned softly, taking a large gulp. Dax smiled and watched me contently, sliding his thumb up and down his mug.

"I'm glad you like it." He looked down at the tiled island we sat at and traced the lines.

"What's keeping you up?" I questioned, licking my bottom lip of excess chocolate.

"I was up with Emilia, she had a nightmare. I was leaving her room when I saw you coming into the kitchen." He ran his fingers through his tousled hair.

"Do Darcy and Emilia live here?"

"Yeah, Darcy's husband is in the armed forces and is away a lot. This way Emilia is always with family and Darcy isn't alone." He nodded and took a sip from his mug.

"Wow, that's got to be tough for her."

"It is, but she's strong." Dax smiled down at his cup, caught up in thought.

"This house is beautiful." I noted, looking around at the craftsmanship.

"Yeah, my father built this house with his brothers before he married my mom. It was his wedding gift to her."

"Wow, that's a big gift." I muttered, imagining the amount of time it must have taken craft this house.

"When you find the right woman, you can never do enough to thank her for being yours." He replied quietly, his eyes trained on the tiles.

"How do you know when you've found the right woman?" I turned my head to look at him and he faced me. Dax brought his hand to my cheek and caressed it softly, I closed my eyes and leaned into his gesture, needing his touch more than ever. When I opened my eyes again, Dax's pupils were trained on me in such focus, I began to feel self conscious.

"What?" I looked down shyly, hoping my bedhead didn't look too awful. He tilted my chin upward to meet his eye level.

"I just can't believe how stunning you are." He breathed out, his thumb brushing across my cheek. My heart fluttered, knots forming in my stomach. But reality suddenly came into focus and I realized I couldn't start something with Dax when there was a murderer on the loose with me as his target. Being connected to me put a target on Dax's back as well, and I couldn't do that to him or his family.

"I-I should probably get back to bed." I slipped away from his grip and once my feet felt the cold floor, I padded back toward the guest bedroom. I slipped under the blankets and pulled them over my head, creating a little igloo of self preservation. Pinching my eyes closed, I attempted sleep once again. But with every shift, creak, or sound of wind, my eyes shot open with terror. Dorian Smith slipped into my mind, creeping around the deepest shadows of my imagination. I thought about the possibility of him finding me here and hurting Dax's family, the mere thought of it causing a sob to rush through my chest. Tears flooded from my eyes out of fear and exhaustion. I peeked at the clock on the wall, reading it at three in the morning.

"Jane?" I heard someone call my voice into the room, causing a whimper to slip from my mouth. "Princesa, it's me." A flood of relief soothed my body as the outline of Dax's body came through the darkness.

"Is everything okay?" I whispered softly as I sat up, quickly rubbing my eyes of tears and restlessness.

"I was just about to ask you that, I could hear you crying from my room." He sat on the edge of the bed, "What's wrong?"

"Nothing, I'm fine." I swallowed, making note to cry quieter.

"If only that were believable." He moved forward and the moonlight shown on him, outlining his features in gray scale, his muscles shadowed and glowed under the soft beams.

"I just can't sleep." I shrugged, biting the inside of my cheek. He nodded and placed his hand on my side, squeezing gently.

"Well, I'm right in the next room if you need me." He whispered softly before standing and walking toward the door.

"Please stay," I reached out for him, my throat clenching as a threat of crying. "Please." After a few moments, Dax slipped into the twin sized mattress and situated himself next to me. I laid my head on his bare chest and draped my arm around his waist. And without a word, he snaked his arm around and rubbed small circles into the small of my back.

And without even realizing it, I fell asleep.

17

CHAPTER 17

I woke up just as the sun was rising. A large pair of arms wrapped around me while a muscled body spooned me from behind. Dax was still asleep and I found myself becoming lost in the moment, enjoying the feeling of his warm skin against mine. As time passed by, the sun began to rise and light slowly beamed through the windowpane. My bladder began to shift and I wiggled in discomfort. I didn't want to get out of my safe haven between Dax's arms, but I also didn't want pee on him. So I shimmied out of his hold and tiptoed to the bathroom in Dax's tee shirt that nearly swallowed me whole.

After freshening myself up, I pulled my hair out of the messy bun that it had been tied up in all night. I let my fingers brush through my long brown locks in hopes of untangling some of the mats. As I exited the bathroom, I watched as Dax's arm reached up to send me a peace sign.

"Good morning," I smiled sheepishly, looking down at my bare legs.

"Good morning, Princesa." He mumbled hoarsely, stretching his limbs from beneath the blanket. I leaned against the wall and bit the inside of my cheek, not sure of what to say. He sat up and rubbed sleep away from his eyes, the window adjacent to us allowing beams of morning sunlight into the small room.

Dax

Sleeping next to Jane had been a God-sent. I was able to protect her at a moment's notice while being able to appreciate her from a perspective I had never seen. Having awoken before her, I watched her breathe deeply in her sleep, her nose twitching slightly in tranquil slumber. I was able to see her long eyelashes and how they splayed across the very edge of her upper eyelid. I was able to see the soft freckles that peppered her tanned skin, dancing across her cheeks and nose as if Van Gogh himself had painted each one with care and purpose. Her lip - oh Lord, her lips. Her bottom lip more full than the top, but both gorgeously pink and desirable. It took every inch of willpower not to press mine against hers. To feel her.

When she woke, I quickly pretended to sleep. And when she quietly tiptoed to the bathroom, I let out a deep sigh of relief. I didn't know what was going on between Jane and me, and quite frankly I didn't want to explore it right now. My job was to protect this woman, not seduce her and make her my own. But fuck, I wanted to.

Jane walked out of the bathroom and I attempted to act cool and collect, despite being anything but. And I swallowed hard at the sight of her in my shirt. It engulfed her small frame, ending around mid-thigh where I so badly wanted to drag my teeth against her skin. A sinful image of me springing out of the twin sized mattress to take her in my arms and throw her on the bed, effectively ripping the Calvin Klein fabric down the middle and ravaging her until her toes curled in ecstasy plagued my mind. I shook the thought away.

"Good morning." She looked down at her feet and I took a deep breath. Did she know what she was doing to me? What she always does to me? Her innocence drove me wild and the most primal urge in my body wanted me to destroy it, to fill her with something a little more tangible.

"Good morning, Princesa." I made a mental note to take my frustration to the shower, so I stretched my arms and legs, and rubbed the crust away from my eyes. I knew that my shorts hung low on my hips, but I made no attempt to remedy that fact because I was going to take them off soon anyway. But when I caught Jane's eyes following the trail down my v-line, I smirk flowered on my lips. All thoughts of my job flew out the window. "I'm going to take a shower, then I'll take you down for breakfast."

"O-Oh, okay, yeah, have fun." Jane sputtered out, still watching me as I walked into the bathroom. I closed the door three-quarters of the way shut, leaving it ajar enough to see the mirror.

Jane

I shook my head, trying to gather my thoughts. My god, I can't take this. I felt like I was going to burst out of my skin. If Dax would've touched me, even if it were the most innocent tap on the shoulder, I probably would've moaned. He had to be doing this on purpose because who in the world just looks like that? To avoid any further sexual frustration, I looked through the duffel bag of clothes Dax had packed for me. Sun dresses, shorts, tank tops, sleeveless blouses. He definitely made sure I was taken care of. To make sure I was safe to change without interruption, I approached the bathroom door to make sure the shower was on. Sure enough, the water was running and I let out a sigh of relief. But before I could get away, I accidentally looked into the mirror which was reflecting the sight of Dax's naked body.

"Holy shit." I gasped quietly, ogling the curvature of his tattooed backside. I rarely ever swore, but I saw this situation fit for a good curse word. Heat pooled at my core and my vocal cords let out an involuntary whine of frustration.

I quickly got dressed in a pair of white jean shorts and a blue tie-dyed tank top. Dax exited the shower, sporting a white cotton towel around his waist, to which I faced the other way.

"Good shower?" I questioned, trying to seem as innocent as possible. No, I hadn't just witnessed nicest bottom my eyes have ever beheld.

"Wonderful," He nodded and strode toward the door, his hand on the knob. "I'm going to get some clothes and then we can get some breakfast."

"Take your time." I whispered as he closed the door behind him. It took Dax just minutes to find an ensemble that made him look completely jaw dropping. In a plain white oversize tank top and black Chino shorts, he smiled at me through the doorway of the guest bedroom.

"Hungry?"

You have no idea.

18

CHAPTER 18

When we entered the kitchen, the Rivera family was in full swing. Emilia was in a highchair, squishing different pieces of fruit with a plastic spoon. Dax's mother, who I was informed to call Dia, was frying eggs in a large cast iron pan on the stove while simultaneously flipping tortillas on a warmer. Darcy was stirring a large pot of rice, also multitasking with stirring a pan of black beans. A man I had not been introduced to was cutting tomatoes, limes, avocados, and peppers skillfully with a knife. Dax's face lit up at the sight of the man.

"Papá!" Dax exclaimed as the man stood, embracing Dax in a warm hug.

"Hijo mío, es bueno verte." Dax's father smiled happily, and I wondered why I hadn't met him yesterday with the rest of the family.

"Ha pasado demasiado tiempo." The embraced again before Dax turned to me, ready to introduce me. "Papá, esta es Jane, la chica de la que hablamos por teléfono." Dax's father reached for me and I placed my hand in his. The man pressed a kiss to my skin and smiled lovingly.

"My name is Emilio Rivera, it is a pleasure to meet you." He then shook my hand and gently let it go. "I was told you do not speak Spanish, why is that?"

"Papá," Dax said warningly, but his father waved him off disconcertingly.

"Oh, well, my parents' ancestors were from France, so I was taught French." I bit my lip, feeling everyone's eyes on me.

"I was unaware you spoke French, Princesa." Dax leaned in to whisper in my ear. "I'd love to hear it sometime." My cheeks scorched red and hot.

"Well, how interesting. Come, sit." Emilio insisted, pulling out a chair for me. Taking the seat, I scooted into the table and folded my hands in my lap. Plates of food were dished out and I tried Huevos Rancheros for the first time. Mexican cuisine was different than what I had growing up in a French family. French food was often light and delicate, served with wine and some sort of aged cheese. I found Mexican food to be dense with savory flavors, with emphasis on meat and vegetables. I loved both.

"Daxon says you go to University in the States, what is your major?" Darcy asked, feeding her daughter a piece of avocado.

"Veterinary science." I nodded simply, taking a drink of milk. "I love animals."

"That's wonderful," Dia shook her head in amazement. "Your parents must be very proud." At the mention of my parents, Dax's hand found mine under the table, squeezing gently to comfort me. I smiled softly in thanks to him and nodded to his mother.

"I hope so." The rest of breakfast went by in a breeze. I had forgotten how wonderful it was to have a meal with family. When everyone had finished eating, Dax offered to do the dishes and I was in charge of drying. We did our chore in silence, both of us looking out of the window that sat in front of the sink. It had been so quiet that I jumped when Emilio reentered the kitchen.

"Daxon, cuando termines los platos, necesito tu ayuda en el campo." Dax nodded to his father and I elbowed his side softly.

"Please tell me you're not leaving me." I pouted, drying the last dish and placing it on the rack. Dax pulled the towel from my fingers and dried his hands, smiling softly.

"I'm sorry, Princesa. I'm afraid so," He leaned against the counter and I followed suit against the island. We stared silently at each other before Dax took a step forward. "But before I go help my father, I'd love to hear you speak a little French." He placed his hands on either side of me, keeping me pinned against the island, like a cornered criminal.

"Vous avez un cul délicieux." I whispered softly, a girlish smile playing on my lips.

"What a beautiful language," Dax mumbled softly, dipping his head down and grazing his lips down the length of my throat, causing my eyes to flutter closed. "Such a pretty mouth, such a foul tongue." My eyes flew open in horror, watching as

Dax pushed himself away from the island and started toward the exit of the kitchen. "If my ass is so scrumptious, Princesa, next time: take a bite." He left me in his family kitchen, jaw practically on the floor in sheer mortification.

"He speaks French, too?" I gasped, covering my eyes as if they could hide me away. Darcy found me like this, and again, I jumped at her presence.

"I'm sorry, did I scare you?" She chuckled softly and patted my shoulder, "Is everything okay?"

"Yeah, your brother's just full of surprises." I laughed shakily, glancing out of the window to find he and his father walking toward the field behind the house.

"Dax can be quite the character," She nodded in agreement, "Are you two...?"

"Oh, no!" I blurted out quickly, "Not really, I mean, it's confusing." Darcy smiled knowingly and took nudged me with her shoulder.

"What do you say about going into town with me? I'll have my mother watch Emilia." Darcy suggested, excitement dancing in her eyes.

"I don't know, last time I went out with one of Dax's sisters, I ended up with a massive hangover." I laughed, wondering what Dalila and Vivian were doing right now.

"Don't worry, I'm the good sister. We'll go shopping and get lunch," She put her hands together to mock praying, "Please?" After deliberating for a moment, I shrugged.

"Why not?" I smiled and Darcy clapped her hands in victory. Who knows how long Dax would be away with his father. Sure, I was in witness protection, but who says I can't have a little fun? Maybe I'll find a souvenir to take back home for Vivian. Besides, I needed a break from Dax anyway. The constant sexual attraction was beginning to drain me of energy. Hanging out with Darcy is exactly what I need and I hope that when I come back, I'll be able to handle myself around her brother.

19

CHAPTER 19

Darcy drove an old silver pick-up truck with soft music playing in the cab. She was right, she was the 'good' sister. Darcy preferred starting a family over the nightlife like Dalila had chosen, she fell in love and married young, following in the footsteps of her mother and father. She talked about her husband like she was the sun and he was the moon; in love, but never close enough to each other. They had been high school sweethearts before he joined the army, and before he shipped out, they married and conceived Emilia.

"So tell me honestly, because Dax hasn't given us a real answer," Darcy said as she parked and hopped out of the truck holding several burlap bags. "Why are the two of you here?" I followed suit, hopping out of the truck and following her down the sidewalk.

"I needed to get away, Dax has been helping me out," I sighed softly, running my fingers through a knot in my hair. "He's been a good friend."

"Friend?" Darcy eyed me suspiciously. "You don't have to give me a cover story, you know. I see the way you two look at each other."

"I'm serious, we're just friends. It's never been more than that for us." I shrugged, looking at my feet as we approached the vendors.

"I've got a gift for these types of things, Jane. My brother's path crosses with yours somewhere, the only question is: when." Darcy began to shop and I followed behind, watching her appraise vegetables and fruits of different array, paying for them before slipping each into her burlap bags. Our last stop was a butcher shop where different kinds of meat were refrigerated and hung for display. Darcy expertly explained the type of meat and cut she expected from the butcher, to which he delivered to her wrapped in a white paper. Slipping the last item into her bag, we began our stroll back to her truck when I passed a quaint shop that sold little souvenirs.

"Can we go in here quickly, I saw something I like." I pleaded with Darcy who nodded.

"Yes, but it needs to be fast, this meat is going to spoil in the heat." I nodded and made my way into the store with Darcy on my heel. I found the table that occupied the item I had seen through the window. I picked up the silver Victorian era comb replica that had been embellished with turquoise stones. "Oh wow, Jane. That's beautiful." Darcy remarked over my shoulder.

"It is." I agreed, biting my lip in deliberation of its purchase.

"I bet my brother would love to see you wear it."

Dax

I hated working in the field with my father. Between the heat and the hard labor, you were exposed to near heat stroke every day. How my father managed to do this work all of his life, I did not know. Because he had my help, we finished the farm work in just a few hours. We had come in for a rest and a drink, my mother pouring us both a glass of lemonade when I realized I had not seen Jane yet.

"Mamá, ¿dónde está Jane?" I questioned, looking between her and my father.

"Creo que se fue con Darcy." Mom shrugged and drank a glass of lemonade herself, relaxing after a day of housework. But I was anything but lax. I sprang out of my chair and ran to my bedroom to grab my cell phone. I dialed Darcy's number, only to be put through to voicemail. I called and called, and called. If anything bad happened to Jane, I would never forgive myself. An hour went by and I paced the hallway that lead to the front door. My parents had ceased asking what was wrong, because I gave no answer.

After another twenty minutes, the sound of tires on gravel filled my ears. I whipped the front door open and sprinted toward my sister's truck. Darcy was the first to exit the cab, pulling bags of produce with her. I sent her an angry look before darting to the passenger side and ripping the door open. Jane cowered within the cab, watching me in confusion.

"Where the fuck have you been?" I yelled, allowing her to exit the cab, slamming the door behind her. She frowned at me and looked to Darcy for help, but my sister had already run into the house for protection. "Jane." I ground her name out between my clenched teeth.

"Darcy asked me to go to the market with her, you were busy so I didn't see anything wrong with-"

"You didn't see anything wrong with going out?" I questioned, laughing cynically. "How about, Dorian Smith is on our ass trying to find you? What if something happened, Jane? I wouldn't be there to protect you!" My chest heaved with anger and worry, veins pulsing in my forehead and neck.

"Nothing happened!" She yelled back at me, her fists balled at her sides. I took in the sight of her. Her big, gorgeous amber eyes watching me angrily. How beautiful her hair was, flowing down her body in waves of chocolate; a silver comb displayed in contrast of her dark locks. It pissed me off to no end that she could be so stupid as to go off in a place she's never been when a murderer was on a hunt for her. I could feel my rage billowing off of me, but I didn't care if she knew I was angry with her.

"You know what, Jane?" I growled, backing her against the cab of the truck, placing my hands on either side of her to prevent escape.

"What?" She yelled back at me, obviously too angry at me to care about anything else.

"You know what?" I said again, feeling my anger shift to something else.

"What, Dax?" She hissed, looking up at me. Without hesitation, I smashed my lips to hers, one of my hands lifting to hold her jawline in place. To my surprise, Jane quickly melted into the kiss, throwing her hands in my hair and tugging gently. My thoughts went to the night at the club when we kissed, but this was so much different. She was sober and she wanted this. I pressed my body against hers, needing to feel her against me, never wanting her to be any farther from me than this. Her lips parted in a moan against mine and I took imitative to deepen the kiss. Her lips felt like silk against me, my hand drifted from her jaw to her cheek, knowing the kiss was about to end. I slid my thumb across her cheekbone gently and leaned my forehead against hers, both of us breathing harshly as we parted.

"Wow." She whispered as I pressed my forehead against her's.

"Wow."

20

CHAPTER 20

The noise of yelling and laughter caused me to toss and turn in the early morning. I groaned and slapped my hands against the pillows, pushing myself up and out of bed. Slipping into my robe, I stumbled down the stairs and found myself following the noise to the family room. Dax was surrounded by three men, all of them standing at similar statures and build. It must be true that attractive people stick together; all four men in front of me could've been mistaken for models. When I entered the room, they stopped talking and turned to look at me. I shifted from one foot to the other uncomfortably under their stare.

"Oh, amigo mío, ¿has traído un pequeño regalo para nosotros?" One of them directed toward Dax, stepping forward to intercept me. He offered his hand to me and I hesitantly took it, shortly before I felt a familiar arm grab my waist and pull me backward. My backside met with Dax's front as he placed a firm grip on my hip, keeping me in place at his side.

"Esta es Jane, mantendrás tus manos alejadas de ella, todos ustedes." Dax nearly growled, his grip on me tightening slightly.

I bit my lip, feeling out of the loop among the ethnic men and their conversation. Although I was beginning to pick up on some Spanish, I still would get lost in conversations longer than a couple of sentences. Dax's attention refocused on me, his thumb rubbing a gentle circle into the fabric of my robe.

"Jane, these are my best friends: Angel," The man whose hand I had almost shook waved with a smile. He stood just a few inches shorter than Dax, his hair pressed into a Nike baseball hat while he sported a black v-neck tee and a pair of maroon Chino shorts. "Benito," A man behind Angel popped his head out as his name was called. His skin was a chocolate brown color, his eyes a warm amber. Benito wore a pair of black jeans and white t-shirt that had something printed in Spanish.

"Call me Benny." He stated with a smile accompanied by a cheeky wink.

"And last, but not at all least: Chris." The last man took a step forward, but what surprised me about him was that he was wearing a military uniform.

"It's a pleasure meeting you, Jane," He patted Dax on the shoulder, "I'll catch up with you some more later, I need to see my wife." He slipped past Dax and me, and walked down the hallway. Pieces of the puzzle started to fit together just as I heard a scream come from the other end of the house.

"I called in a few favors to have Chris home for a of couple days," Dax chuckled, "I thought it'd be more fun to surprise Darcy than to have her in on it." I grinned, my heart warming with his loving sentiment toward his family and their happiness.

"I can't believe one of your best friends ended up with your sister," I whispered to him in disbelief.

"That how they met, actually; through me. He pursued her from the time we were fifteen to seventeen, until she finally gave him a pity date - which worked out well, as you can see." He nodded toward a frame on the wall that held a photograph of Darcy and Chris on their wedding day.

"Oh shit, we've got to run," Angel knocked elbows with Benny, "We'll see you tonight though, D." Before anyone could say goodbye's, the two men were out of the door. I cocked an eyebrow up at Dax as he turned me around to face him.

"D?"

"Oh, yeah," He chuckled throatily, "Our nickname in high school was the ABCD's. Angel was A, Benny was B, Chris was C, and I was obviously D." He placed his warm hand against my cheek, cupping my jawline gently. I leaned into his touch, fluttering my eyes closed in comfort. "They're putting a party together to celebrate me coming home," He placed a soft butterfly kiss to the base of my throat, "Come?"

By early evening, Dax had been called away by his friends to come to the party they had thrown for him. I opted for coming later with Darcy and Emilia, knowing she was the only person I was going to be talking to while Dax was busy catching up with everyone. When I walked into her bedroom, she looked me up and down with a frown.

"You're wearing that?" She raised an eyebrow. I looked down at my outfit in confusion. A pair of shorts and a nice shirt didn't seem awful to me. So when I shrugged, she rolled her eyes and rushed to her closet. "You've never been to a party down here, let me help you out." She grinned at something she had found and turned to me. "Put this on." I looked at the short hem and thin straps in utter horror.

"No way, I'm sorry but no." I shook my head multiple times to convey my absolute answer. She pouted at me, putting her hands together in mock praying. "No, Darcy, no!"

Darcy was bursting with giddy joy was we walked up to the lit up barn just a few miles from the Rivera household. White fairy lights had been strung across the top of the building and led to the entrance. By the amount of cars parked in the field, there must have been hundreds of people coming to this party. Butterflies began to swarm in my belly, a light sheen of sweat spreading to my back. I stopped short of the entrance and debated whether I should go in or not.

"Are you okay, Jane?" She asked, watching me in worry.

"Yeah, yeah," I laughed shakily. "It's just... there's a lot of people and I don't know if this dress is really complimenting my body type-"

"I'm going to stop you right there. You look super hot, okay? There's no way that Dax or any other guy will be able to take their eyes off of you." She smiled and took my hand, gently tugging me forward, "Trust me." So I followed her inside, finding the barn was completely renovated into a dance space, with hardwood floors, a bar, and a DJ. I spotted Dax from across the room wearing a white button up dress shirt with the sleeves rolled up to his elbows, his lower half sporting a pair of black straight-legged Chinos. I looked down at my outfit one last time, attempting to gain confidence before I forced myself to walk in his direction. Darcy shot me a smile before leading the way. I felt my straightened hair fall down my back, the heels Darcy had borrowed me clicked against the floor, announcing my presence.

Dax

I took a small drink from the bottle in my hand while my friends brought me up to speed on what had happened in the last two years I had been gone. I missed them, I missed this. When I had lived here in my youth, nights were always like this. Simple.

"Obviamente no invitamos a Camila-" Angel stopped short, his eyes and what seemed to be everyone else's, were on something else. Someone else. I turned to their line of sight, my eyes catching with hers. Straight dark brown hair shining under the light of the barn we had rebuilt as teenagers, her lips glossed and glowing like a delectable piece of dessert. My eyes defied my honorable judgement and slipped down her body. The white dress clung to her mesmerizing curves like it depended on them.

"Mierda." I whispered, trying to snap out of my trance.

"La pequeña mamá tiene un culo" Benny chuckled, to which I had to resist the urge to punch him in the mouth. I strode forward, my jaw clench as drew nearer. Taking a deep breath, my insides melted in reaction to her scent and I wanted to get lost in it. She smiled shyly up at me, her hands folded together innocently in front of her, causing her cleavage to practically spill out of the low cut ensemble.

"Por el amor de Dios." I grumbled, pulling her hands apart and placing them at her sides. Her eyes searched my face in confusion, but I quickly pulled her away from the main crowd. She struggled to keep up with me in heels that I didn't remember packing for her, what happened to all the shorts and t-shirts I had packed for her? Where did this come from? We came to an ill lit corner of the barn and I struggled to keep my thoughts together.

"What are you wearing?" I manage to choke out, biting my lip.

"I was wearing something else, but Darcy didn't think I would fit in wearing what I had picked out so she borrowed this to me for tonight," She looked down at her feet, "It looks bad, doesn't it." I let out a shaky breath, laughing to myself in disbelief.

"Are you kidding? You look fucking- You... I-" I shook my head, "Indescribable." A smile replaced the sad pout that had been on her lips.

"Is Officer Rivera lost for words?" She teased, poking my chest. I caught her finger with my hand and grabbed her waist with my free one, pulling her into me.

"Ms. Kingsley, I wouldn't play with me right now, I'm not opposed to a strip search." I mumbled huskily into her ear. I felt her shiver under my touch and I smirked, grazing my lips across her collarbone.

"Oh, isn't this charming?" A voice claimed from behind me. My mouth instantly contorted into a scowl and Jane had noticed, craning her neck around me to see who had spoken. But I didn't have to turn around to see her. I knew her voice well enough to place it to a face.

"Camilia." I sighed, turning on my heel so that Jane was behind me.

"Hello, Daxon." She sent me a sugary smile and I snorted.

"Who is that?" Jane asked from behind me, my muscles tightening at her question. I never thought I'd have to bring up Camilia to Jane, and I found myself searching for the right term.

"Sweetie, I'm his ex-fiance." Camilia waved to Jane in a mock-friendly manner. And suddenly I was between them; on one side, a woman I had a long complicated history with and on the other, the woman I wanted more than anything in the world.

"Dax, tell me that's not true." Jane pleaded, her eyes desperate.

"It's true." I sighed, reaching for her, "Let me explain-"

"I need a drink." Jane brushed past me to the bar, several male eyes following her as she walked.

"I think it's time we caught up, Daxon." Camilia purred from behind me, "It's been too long."

21

CHAPTER 21

J ane

I sulked at the bar for half an hour before Darcy and Dax's friends found me. After I had told them what had happened, Darcy sighed sympathetically and moved a few strands of hair away from my face.

"I'm sorry, Jane. Camilia is a part of Dax's past that he's not proud of, which is why he probably never told you about her." She rubbed my back comfortingly.

"Puta ruined his life down here." Angel glowered over at them. Dax and Camilia had been talking since I had left for a drink, neither of them paying any mind to the fact I was now absent. I couldn't help but watch the way she held herself; confident, sexy, and alluring. She was, undoubtedly beautiful with big green eyes, plump lips, a thin waist and big butt.

"Don't worry about her, Jane. She's bad news, but Dax hates her; we all do." Benny noted begrudgingly. I looked between Dax's friends, cocking an eyebrow.

"Is there something you guys want to share?" The men looked at each other and then back to me.

"Camilia was the hottest girl in our high school, everyone wanted her and she took advantage of that. During our senior year, Camilia made her way through our group." Benny grimaced.

"Meaning...?"

"Angel, Benny, and Dax slept with her." Darcy interjected with a shrug, sipping at her drink through a straw.

"We hated each other, all of us competing for her like she was a prize. We took her on dates, bought her whatever she asked for. But it was never enough." Angel grumbled plopping down into the chair next to me. "She finally picked Dax and he was obviously so manipulated into thinking what they had was love, that he proposed to her. A couple of months later, she found out she was pregnant," I felt bile begin to rise in my throat.

"Please tell me Dax does not have a child with her." My hand covered my mouth in case I needed to vomit.

"That was the thing, Camilia pops and to everyone's surprise: the baby was a lot darker than expected." I looked between the three of them in confusion, before finding Benny's head lowered in guilt.

"No," I gasped, "It's yours?"

"Sadly, the mother of my child is a major puta, but I got a son out of it so I can't complain." He shrugged, finishing Angel's drink for him.

"Wow," I shook my head in disbelief. "So what happened?"

"Dax broke off the engagement, the three of us mended our friendship and he went to the States to be a do-gooder," Benny took my hand and kissed it. "You have nothing to worry about from Camilia, just talk to Dax."

"I know I should, I just need a couple moments to myself." I sighed and between the side hugs and empathetic back pats, they left me to my thoughts. Only a few minutes had gone by when I felt him behind me. His presence felt safe and comforting but I couldn't shake the feeling of jealousy I felt for Camilia.

"I'm sorry." He whispered from behind me, "I should have told you about Camilia, it's just hard for me to bring her up. I thought I loved her, but I didn't. I didn't know what love was, but now-" I spun in my chair to face him.

"Dax, I just need a few minutes alone to think. I'm not mad at you and truthfully I have no reason to be, it was before we met." I sighed softly and looked up into his sorrowful eyes. "I'm just... shocked."

"Understandable," He cleared his throat. "Well, when you are done thinking, please come find me, we have to talk." He pressed a soft kiss to my cheek and disappeared into the crowd. I felt tears drip into my line of sight and I made a lame attempt to stop them from falling. I pushed off of my seat and made my way toward the exit.

"Jane, are you okay?" I heard Dax's mother call to me, to which I simply nodded and ran faster. Once outside, I placed my hand against my chest and slumped against the wall of the barn. I shouldn't be this hurt over something that happened before I knew Dax, it was childish of me to be this upset. The worst part of me became anxious, finding the depths of insecurities and comparing them to Camilia.

She is prettier than me. She is more confident than me. She has had him.

Dax

Someone tapped on my shoulder as I ordered myself another whiskey, neat. I turned, finding my mother wearing her best jewelry and a new dress. Her hand drifted from my shoulder to my forearm, squeezing it warmly. I smiled as best as I could manage, feeling sunken from my conversation with Jane.

"Mijo, what are doing?," She looked into my eyes and I looked into hers. Those green orbs mirrored my own and held many years of wisdom, motherly and otherwise.

"¿Qué quieres decir?" I questioned before thanking the bartender for my drink. ["What do you mean?"]

"I don't understand the two of you, one moment you're out in my driveway besándose and the next, she's running out of the room crying," She grabbed my chin firmly, "Fix this." I shook my head and took a sip from my glass.

"She said she wants a couple minutes alone." She laughed softly at my response, patting my shoulder.

"Oh Mijo, you have fallen into a trap many men fail to get out of. She doesn't want you to leave her alone, she wants you to go after her."

"But-"

"Créeme." She patted my cheek lovingly, pushing me gently toward the exit. ["Trust me."]I nodded, feeling a rush of adrenaline run through me as I attempted to pump myself up. It wasn't every day that I professed my feelings to someone, much less Jane. I left the bar and ignored Angel's calls to indulge in a round of shots with him, looking for any sign of Jane. I pushed through the exit and and made my way around the side of the barn, finding her small figure hidden away by a shadow. The sun was in it's last few moments of setting, the sky a medley of orange, red, and blue, sprinkled with stars that reminded me of Jane's freckles. I made my way over to her, giving her little time to react to my presence.

"I was stupid," I took a small gulp before I continued, "I was a stupid teenager, Jane. She made me compete for her attention and I thought, because I won, that what we had was love. Camilia put me through hell and you know what? I'm glad. I'm glad because the hell she put me through led me to become an officer in the States, which led me to Wisconsin; which led me to you. And I have never felt-" My voice broke off and my head dropped. It suddenly felt as though the weight of a thousand bricks had fallen on my shoulders. Jane watched me closely, her eyes welled and searching for the rest of my sentence. "I have never felt for anyone the way I feel about you." She swallowed and I became silent, listening to the heavy heartbeat in my ears. After a few moments of silence, she took a step forward and slid her hand across my jawline, pulling me down to her level. Barely a second had flown by, but everything seemed to be in slow motion. Jane pressed her lips against mine, and I slowly melted into the surprising gesture. When she pulled away, I felt breathless. I looked down at her, a permanent smile on my face.

"Stop it," Her cheeks burnt red; I loved that. When I didn't stop smiling, she smacked my chest with her palm playfully and rolled her eyes.

"I can't." I replied honestly, my cheeks even aching from my facial muscle use. Jane leaned into my chest and I welcomed her warmth, despite the temperature. "Do you want to get out of here?"

"Please."

22

CHAPTER 22

Jane

Dax drove us back to his family home. He helped me out of the passenger seat and led the way through the front door. With neither of us having a plan, we slipped into the kitchen to make something to eat. Dax recovered a frozen pizza from the depths of his parent's freezer to which we both agreed wouldn't be so bad. Dax slip the cheese pizza into the oven and close the door quickly. Leaning against the counter, I watched him move in front of me and dip his head down, catching my lips with his own. I melted into the kiss immediately, wrapping my arms around his neck in attempt to climb to his eye level. To assist me, Dax wrapped his large hands around the underside of my thighs and lifted me onto the counter. He stepped between my legs and leaned his forehead against the exposed skin of my chest, his warm breath traveling down the cleavage of my dress. An army of goosebumps rose across my skin and I shivered involuntarily.

We were silent, but it didn't matter. I looked down at Dax with emotions that I didn't recognize in my eyes, my head spinning. I needed him to make the first move, but I knew he wanted to do things at my pace, which ruined any chance of him taking charge. So when he finally lifted his head to meet my gaze, I was surprised when he took my hand and helped me slide off of the island.

"Come with me." He mumbled softly into my hair as he pressed a sweet kiss to my temple. I nodded, confused at his behavior. Dax never struck me as the type to be gentle; hell, I witnessed him having sex and he was anything but. Yet he was suddenly taking things slow and it made me feel inadequate. I followed him to a room I had never seen and when he opened the door, a small smile played on my lips.

I was in Dax's childhood bedroom.

My eyes scanned the walls, finding old rock band posters pinned to the walls, pictures of young Dax with his friends and family in frames hung and displayed like art. I grinned at a specific picture of Dax as a teenager, just coming into manhood with scrawny arms and legs.

"What happened to this kid," I teased, glancing back at him with a coy smile.

"Hey, not all of us come gorgeous straight from the womb like you, Princesa." He said from behind me.

"Oh stop, you were such a cutie."

"And now?" He questioned, the playful edge to his voice becoming evident.

"You're alright..." I turned to face him, a cheeky smile on my lips. Dax strode forward, shaking his head and laughing lightly.

"Well I'm honored that you think so highly of me, nena." He mumbled, his hand cupping my jawline while his thumb brushed across my cheekbone.

"Nena?" I questioned, biting the inside of my cheek, "What does nena mean?"

"Babygirl." He answered simply. It was one word, three syllables. Yet suddenly, my core was burning with need, radiating outward as my skin began to warm. I stretched onto my tiptoes and attempted to kiss him passionately, but because of my small stature compared to his giant status, I merely pecked his lips. Dax chuckled and craned his neck, eliminating the distance for me to kiss him the way I needed to. In my second try, Dax kissed me back fervently, backing me against the wall. My fingers disappeared in his soft dark brown locks, pulling and tugging gently at the roots. Dax's tongue flirted with my bottom lip and I obliged, parting my lips to deepen the kiss. I moaned into his mouth, feeling lightheaded and hungry for more.

-Mature content below, read at your own discretion-

"We can stop whenever you want," Dax whispered softly and I smiled, taking his hand in mine.

"Dax," I used his fingers to gently slip the thin straps of my dress down my arm. "I don't want to stop." With a nod, Dax leaned down and pressed a soft kiss to my lips while his hands pulled the entirety of my dress off. His eyes bore into mine as he placed my hands on his chest. I slowly unbuttoned his shirt until it hung loosely on his shoulders. He shrugged it off and kissed down my neck, his tongue gliding over my collarbones painstakingly slow. Finding the clothing ratio between us to be far less on my part, I slowly pulled his belt through the loops of his Chinos and let it fall to the floor. My fingertips flicked the button of his pants through the hole and he helped me pull them off of his legs. The moment seemed so intense, we were breathing so hard and yet we had done nothing but take each other's clothes off.

"I don't think we ever talked about this, but I've never done this." I swallowed hard, anticipating some sort of crazy reaction. Dax was quiet for a moment, his bottom lip caught between his teeth in thought.

"Well, I'm not going to lie, I don't hate the idea of me being the only guy you will have been with," I rolled my eyes and smacked his chest. He laughed quietly and leaned his forehead against mine, "Are you ready for this?"

"Yes." I answered instantly, not a single thought having to pass my mind to know the answer to that question. Without another word, Dax continued to kiss down my body, coming back to where he had left off right between my cleavage. Dax dropped to his knees, his eyes now level with my breasts.

"Hermosa [Beautiful]." He whispered, his breath hitting my nipples and causing them to firm. A soft sigh escaped my mouth and I fluttered my eyes closed while Dax blew cool air against the hardened buds. I almost ached with need and not long after, Dax's warm mouth enveloped my nipple, his teeth skimming the bud, his tongue quickly soothing the bite. I whimpered, my fingers pulling at his hair for more. Dax then moved to my left nipple, his tongue working and swirling around it with the same vigor as he had my right. With one last kiss applied to the wet skin, Dax's tongue slipped down my navel, his teeth gently tugging at the lace of my underwear. He looked up at me, his eyes trained on me as he slowly tugged them down. I took a deep breath, enjoying the sensation of his breath against my sex. With his eyes still looking into mine, Dax spread my legs and licked up my inner thighs. I knew I was already wet and I could feel him smirk against me, his tongue inching closer and closer to where I needed him to be. And almost as if he could read my mind, his tongue jutted out and licked up my folds. I spluttered out an incoherent jumble of letters, unable to connect any fragment of higher thinking. Finding my cl!t, Dax gently nipped at the bundle of nerves before his tongue ran circles around it vigorously. My mouth involuntarily formed in the shape of an 'o' and my fingers dug into his shoulders, my knees beginning to buckle from beneath me.

"Delicioso." He murmured, causing vibrations to rack through my throbbing sex. Going south, his tongue suddenly eased into my entrances, curling its length inside of me. My back arched and I whimpered his name, my eyes welling. His mastered tongue pumped in and out of me while his thumb worked my cl!t, causing me to shake and writhe from above him. My knees began to feel like gelatin, wobbling like a new-born and about to give out. As I began to fall, Dax caught my thighs and lifted me against the wall, my legs now wrapped around his waist. "Tell me how that felt, Princesa." He mumbled as he kissed across my shoulder, sucking love bites into the skin.

"I-I-" I swallowed, my head still spinning. "G-Good." Dax smiled against my jaw and opened up the nightstand beside him, pulling out a golden foil package. With one arm support-ing me, Dax slipped his boxer briefs down his legs and I felt his member graze against my backside.

"Do you want to keep going?" He asked, searching my eyes for any signs of discomfort.

"Please." I nodded, taking the foil package from his hand and ripping it open. "S'il vous plait, Monsieur. [Please, sir.]" Dax's normally bright green eyes darkened as I spoke French to him, his grip on me tightening. The latex slipped onto Dax's member and he situated himself below me, his tip slicking between my folds. I looked into his eyes as he slowly push in, my walls tightening around him. He groaned lowly, biting his lip to control himself.

"Te sientes tan jodidamente bien. [You feel so fucking g ood.]" He growled, taking a deep breath. Once he had his hips pressed to mine, he waited for me to give him a sign to move. It took a few moments for me to adjust to not only the intrusion, but his size. After awhile the pain melted into a delicious burn and I nodded for him to continue. He recoiled and thrust again, this time slightly faster. With each thrust, the sensations began to shift from painful to earth-shattering pleasure. My hips began to buck against his in attempt to push him to go faster, harder, deeper. His fingers dug into the skin of my ass as my nails scraped down his muscled back. I kissed him hard, tasting myself on his tongue as he fucked into me. Our hips met and divided over and over, causing sounds to echo throughout his bedroom. Without missing a beat, Dax carried me to his bed and threw me onto the firm mattress before grabbing my legs and pulling me to the foot of the bed. He threw my legs over his shoulders and plunged back into my entrance, grazing something within me that made me see stars.

"Juste là, s'il vous plaît ne vous arrêtez pas, monsieur. [Just there, please do not stop, sir.]" I cried out, my head thrown back and my spine arched. Dax readjusted himself to another angle that managed to hit that specific spot repeatedly, my core swirling in a pit of heat and satisfaction. I fisted the sheets, Dax's name falling from my lips in the form of moans on repeat.

"I'm close, I'm close," I whined softly, to which Dax licked his thumb and began to rub figure-eights against my cl!t.

"Déjalo ir, nena. [Let go, baby girl.]" He grunted into each thrust, encapsulating one of my nipples in his mouth. My core built and built, and built until finally I shattered, my legs becoming noodles as my toes curled in ecstasy. Dax rode out my orgasm, my walls tightening around his c!ck, bringing him to his climax. With one final drive, Dax spilled his seed into the latex inside of me, his chest heaving above my trembling body. I kissed the tattooed muscle, the taste of his sweat solidifying what we had just done. He slowly pulled out of me and discarded the latex in a garbage bin, falling into the bed beside me.

"Wow." Dax said breathily, his eyes on the ceiling.

"Wow." I nodded in agreement, my cheeks red and hot. This was when we finally noticed the black cloud of smoke hovering at the ceiling of Dax's bedroom. We looked at each other in confusion until we remembered: the pizza. Dax quickly pulled on a pair of joggers and ran downstairs to the kitchen. Tired and out of breath, I opted for lazily slipping Dax's dress shirt over my bareness. My eyes caught sight of a shadow shifting in the moonlight and I crawled out of the bed to investigate. Dax's voice boomed from the kitchen, coughing from the amount of smoke. I cocked my head to the side, my heart freezing in my chest as I watched a shadowed figure step forward.

"We haven't officially met, Jane," The man's voice was deep, calm, and collected. "I think it's about time that we do."

23

—·—

CHAPTER 23

I am five and coming home from kindergarten. The day had been fun, I painted and sat on the bus with my best friend, Vivian. I walk up the twisting walkway toward the door of our two story home. White pillars stood proudly, displaying the front door like an entrance to a fantasy world, a gold knocker situated near the top. I push through the door and set my backpack down while kicking my shoes off. Hearing Mommy and Daddy talking in the kitchen, I creep down the hallway to scare them. As I get closer, I begin to make out what they are saying, but I don't understand. Mommy is crying, Daddy is crying.

"He can't do this." Daddy calls out, his voice hoarse and tired.

"He's threatening to bring us to court." Mommy's voice says and I lean against the door to hear them better. A chair moves and I hear footsteps walking around the hardwood of our kitchen floor.

"She's our daughter, we have rights - she has rights." Daddy insists. When Mommy says nothing, Daddy continues, "I was there through the pregnancy, I was there the day she was born, her first word, first step, first day of school-" He broke off as I slipped into the room, unable to listen anymore.

"Daddy, what's wrong?" I questioned, looking between my parents. My father wiped away his tears and opened his arms to me. I eagerly ran into them, squeezing him around his middle.

"Nothing is wrong, Jaybird, everything is okay." I smiled at his nickname for me and kissed his cheek. If my Daddy says things are okay, I don't have to worry.

I awoke from my dream and sat up in the twin sized bed I was laying in. The walls were a sickly green color with blotches of water damage, a single painting of a flower hung on the wall. My heart beat hard in my chest, my breathing becoming erratic. I have no idea where I am and the last thing I remember was someone shoving fabric against my mouth until I fell asleep. The wooden floor was splintered and cracked, with a worn yellow rug topping it off to cover some of the damage. Still dressed in Dax's white dress shirt, I stood and tiptoed to the door, slowly opening it to avoid any creaks or other noises. The coast was clear so I began my escape down the stairs where the smell of food wafted my nostrils. My belly grumbled with hunger as I made my way into what seemed to be a kitchen, a man stood cooking over the stove. From behind, the man looked normal, sporting a pair of jeans and a basic tee, his short silver hair slicked to the side. He flipped something in the pan, whistling a happy tune as he did.

"Good morning," He spoke gingerly, spinning on his heel to face me. "I made breakfast." He plated two eggs and a couple of slices of bacon, setting a fork at its side. I was frozen, my feet unable to move as I watched my kidnapper act so nonchalant. "Please sit." He instructed, pointing to the chair with a spatula, plating his own food. Swallowing dryly, I slowly slid into the chair to avoid making him angry and stared down at the food. A smiley face of breakfast food stared back up at me and I wondered if he positioned them like this on purpose. "I'm sure you have questions." I stayed quiet, my hands folded in my lap, clutching the excess fabric of Dax's long sleeves. "You don't have to be afraid of me, Jane."

"If you want money, I have a trust that's maturing in three years. If I call the bank right now, I'm sure I can get at least half of it matured right now." I promised, my throat closing around each word.

"I don't want your money, Sweetheart." The man smiled almost lovingly toward me. I watched him dumbfounded for a moment, shaking my head. This man had camped out in Dax's bedroom for who knows how long, and most definitely saw us doing adult activities. I squirmed uncomfortably at the thought of his prodding eyes, having had a full view of me losing my virginity to Dax.

"Who are you?" I finally found the courage to look him in the eyes, finding him oddly familiar. He paused for a long moment, swallowing a bite of food he had put into his mouth.

"Dorian Smith." He replied softly, watching my face contort from fear to horror. I stood quickly, the wooden chair falling behind me as I booked for the door. Dorian beat me there, twisting the padlock shut. "Let me explain my side of the story and I think you-"

"You killed my family." I hissed, tears brimming in my eyes. "You killed innocent people; you ruined my life." From behind him, I looked into a sitting room where a window displayed a rugged landscaped with no other buildings in sight. Even if I could get away, where would I go? The shirt I sported smelled like Dax and I sent out a mental SOS to him.

"Please, Jane, just sit down and eat. I will explain everything." Dorian gently grabbed my arm, pulling me back toward the kitchen. Heavy, hot tears rolled down my cheeks.

I was going to die.

Dax

It had been eighteen hours. I glanced at the phone at my temporary desk for the billionth time, hoping some sort of tip would come in, but it hadn't rung once. The San Sebastian Bernal police department had welcomed me into their small facility with open arms. Their small staff was out scouring every building for Jane while my commanding officer order me to stay by the phone in case someone called in with a clue to where she could be. Not only was I pissed that I wasn't out there looking for her myself, but I couldn't help but relive the moment I realized she was gone, over and over as I sat in the silent room. I searched the entire house, called everyone I knew if they had seen her; I drove all night, down every street in hope of finding her. The station's front door opened with a jingle and I raised my head in tired, helpless hope. But instead was met with disappointment.

"Camilia, not now." I groaned, rubbing my eyes. Camilia was falling back into her old antics, keeping tabs on where I was, and coming at me with low cut tops and short skirts. The teenager she had manipulated years ago would've had her on this desk in seconds. But a man in love only has eyes for his girl, and my girl was missing.

"I heard about your little friend," She leaned forward over the desk, pressing her breasts together. "Can I do anything to help?" I averted my eyes, unamused by her bullshit games.

"You can get the fuck out." I pointed to the door, my jaw clenched in irritation. Between the four pots of coffee and no sleep, I had no patience for anyone, much less Camilia.

"Oh D, you don't mean that." She purred, her index fingers tapping the bottom of my chin. I looked into her eyes, searching for that irrational feeling of infatuation I felt as a seventeen year old wrapped around her finger. I found nothing.

"Camilia, I swear, if don't have any information about Jane, I will throw you out on your ass myself." I growled, slamming my fists against the desk. She jumped, taking a step back before looking at her feet.

"I do have information," She muttered, "After I noticed you had left the party, I drove over to your parent's house to see if you had gone home." I watched her intensely, my eyes following her every movement. "And as I was about to pull into the driveway, I saw a man lifting your friend into a car. He drove away really quick."

"Do you remember what kind of car?" I searched rapidly for a radio, finally finding one at the sheriff's desk.

"A yellow Ford Cortina with a dent in the passenger door; the thing looked straight out of the eighties." I quickly called in the tip, telling all units that we were in search for an old yellow Ford Cortina with a dent in the passenger door. After twenty minutes, one of the deputies brought in tapes from local traffic cameras, showing a car that matched Camilia's description. I smiled at the monitor, pausing the tape as I saw a familiar face come into view.

Dorian Smith.

"I've got you now, motherfucker."

24

— ◆ —

CHAPTER 24

D ax
Due to a burglary, the San Sebastian Bernal police force was turned over to domestic affairs and because backup from the States wouldn't be here for a few more hours. Tired of following orders that didn't get me any closer to Jane, I continued the hunt on my own against my commanding officer's instructions. I promised Jane that I wouldn't let anything bad happen to her and I failed to keep that promise, but there was no way in hell I wasn't going to find her. I was able to trace Smith's car to the outskirts of town, but that's where the trail ended, so I followed the only road he could've taken. I drove half an hour with no signs of life anywhere, no buildings or people, not even any animals. The next town wouldn't be for another hour and my anxieties began to eat away at me. Pulling over on the side of the road, I pressed my forehead against the steering wheel and took deep breaths.

"You're going to find her, you're going to find her." I repeated to myself over and over again, until a minuscule amount of my confidence came back. A sign claiming 'private property' peaked my interest and I turned down the long gravel driveway. I drove for several more minutes, finding an old, dingy house hidden behind a rock formation in the middle of no where. Miraculously, the yellow shit car was parked on the side of the house, half covered by a blue tarp. I reversed my car and parked on the road, radioing in my position before slipping my gun into the holster on my hip. Jane was coming out of this alive, even if it meant I wouldn't. I walked the way back to the house, quietly making my way around the perimeter to look for other means of entrance beside the front door. Finding an unlocked cellar, I pulled the doors open and climbed down the rickety cement steps. The odor of mildew penetrated my senses, the pitch black darkness making it hard to stay quiet and undetectable. A swishing noise came from behind me and something hard was cracked over my head, causing my vision to go black.

I woke sometime later, my eyes blurring under the bright white florescence of the cellar, my wrists now locked with chains attached to the floor. None other than Dorian Smith himself stood in front of me, his head cocked to the side with a smug grin plastered on his face. I rolled my head around, my skull aching specifically around my crown from where I'd been hit. I pulled against the chains, my muscles straining against the hard metal with no luck. Dorian had me on my knees, shirtless and vulnerable.

"Welcome, Officer Rivera!" Dorian said giddily, a glint of metal in his hand twinkling in the light. I shook my head to clear my vision, realizing he had a knife. "I've waited some time for this moment. I've thought about it a lot over the past year in prison; should I use a gun? A knife? A rope to hang you up like the dog you are?" He chuckled, shaking his head. "Oh no, I want you to suffer. I want you to know exactly what I went through when I was locked up; the beatings, the starvation, plus a little more."

"Please don't do this," I begged out of breath, "Please don't hurt her."

"Who? Jane?" Dorian laughed loudly, slapping his knee. "Why do you care about her, she's your flavor of the week. Old news by tomorrow."

"I love her." He swallowed, the hot air causing droplets of sweat to cascade down my body.

"I don't give a shit about how you feel," Dorian flipped the knife, catching it by its handle. "Besides, I would never hurt my own daughter." I looked up at him in confusion.

"Jane is not your daughter."

"Oh, but she is my daughter, Detective. Maybe instead of trying to get in her pants, you could do your job." Dorian spat, taking a step near me. "You see, before all of this, I was a professor at the university that Jane's mother attended as a young adult. We had a brief affair, one in which we both claimed to love each other. That is, until that fucking idiot transferred from Chicago." I watched as Dorian's face twisted in jealousy and rage, his knuckles turning white around the handle of the blade. "He stole her from me and it wasn't until months later that I learned she had been pregnant. She made the mistake of coming back to my classroom to collect her things before she graduated, which is when I saw her carrying my child. I was elated, assuming that since we were going to have a baby, it meant we were going to be married and finally start our life together like we had planned. But she took the opportunity to tell me she had already married the man Jane thinks to be her father and that Jane was not mine."

"I don't believe a word of this." I spat, my arms straining against the metal of the chains.

"You don't have to believe me, the documentation proves itself." Dorian recovered a piece of paper from a file, holding it up for me to see. "I did some digging and found the childcare facility Jane was cared as a newborn and stole one of her diapers. I brought it to a lab and received the joyous news seventy-two hours later." The document looked real, a stamp of approval at the top. "I made several attempts to contact Jane's mother, to have a relationship with my daughter. All of which were denied. At one point, I threatened a custody battle, which they counter attacked with telling the judge I had presented explosive anger issues and had poor mental stability."

"So, hypothetically, if all of this is true, what drove you to kill the Kingsley's?" I asked, watching the wheels in his sadistic head turn.

"It was mostly an accident; I had entered their home in the middle of the night in attempt to tell Jane myself, since almost her whole childhood had passed with my absence. When I got to her bedroom, I realized she was gone and ended up tripping on her desk chair in the dark as I was leaving. They found me as I was climbing out of the window and I guess they saw an opportunity. The husband took his shotgun and aimed for my chest, but I quickly rolled back into the house. We fought over the gun and in the mix, it went off. Jane's mother fell to the ground and it felt as though my heart had been ripped out - imagine losing the woman you love right before your eyes. I was so angry, I couldn't be responsible for my actions. I ripped the gun away from him and shot him four times." He paused, a faint smile on his mouth. "I still remember the way his warm blood splattered across my face."

"You're sick." I shook my head, not sure of what to think.

"That may be so, but all of this could have been avoided if they just allowed me to see her in the first place. Now, I'm just making up some long overdue father time." He stepped behind me and gently slid the sharp, cold metal against my throat, a small trickle of blood leaked down my neck. I groaned heavily, hearing him chuckle in my ear. "You're a pathetic piece of shit. I would never let my daughter be with you."

"Yeah, well your daughter calls me daddy, you're third in line now." I smirked at him, his face becoming red as he registered what I had said, earning me a blow across the face. Blood filled from my mouth and I spit it at him as he nursed his hand. My smart mouth wasn't letting me come out of this alive.

25

— ◆ —

CHAPTER 25

J ane

It had been two days. Two days since I found out my entire life was a lie. Two days since I breathed fresh air, saw sunlight, or changed clothes. It had been two days without Dax.

I thought about my mother, how she must have felt finding out she was pregnant by a man she no longer loved. I thought about my father, or at least the man I thought was my father; I remember his love for me, his support, and his belief in me. I yearned for his presence, needing to hear his voice, his advice. My thoughts drifted to Dorian who had driven himself mad over the loss of my mother and then the restricted access to his child. I wanted to escape my own mind for a moment, just for a little while. I cried consistently and refused to eat, despite Dorian bringing me meals at breakfast, lunch, and dinner. At night, I could hear him talking to someone, the sound of him beating some poor human being echoed throughout the house. My only escape from this bedroom was the window, which had been nailed shut and covered with pink drapes. The heat was excruciating and there was no cooling system set up in the house, so I roasted in silence. I couldn't do this anymore, I had sat around and sulked long enough. I needed a plan.

It took me an hour to orchestrate everything. I had tiptoed down to the kitchen where I baked a cake and pulled out a bottle of whiskey I had found under the sink. When Dorian came up the stairs, his hands stained in blood and bruises, I pretended not to see them.

"What is all of this?" Dorian asked from the doorway.

"I know we've never spent Father's Day together, so I thought I'd make up for the years we missed." I forced a smile, presenting him the cake.

"Wow, Sweetheart, I'm touched." Dorian pressed a kiss to my temple. "This looks delicious. Thank you so much." It took me everything not to wipe away the vile kiss, but for the sake of my plan, I smiled through the disgust. We sat down and he sliced the cake while I popped the spun the cap off of the bottle of whiskey. "Whiskey? Isn't that a harsh drink for my little girl?" He pinched my cheek and I laughed cynically.

"I'm just... trying to keep up with my Daddy." I grit through my teeth, pouring both of us a glass. Dorian chuckled, forking the piece of cake into his mouth.

"Your mother was a wonderful baker," Dorian shook his head and sighed, "Too bad." He stood and brought his plate to the sink and I struggled not to pounce on his back, and strangle him right there. When he sat back down, we clinked our glasses together in cheers. I let the alcohol drip down the side of my face that wasn't visible to him, while he downed the entire glass. It continued on like that, the left side of Dax's shirt became saturated in whiskey while Dorian became disoriented, drunk. "You know," Dorian slurred, twirling a few strands of my hair around his finger, "You look just like your mom did when she was young, just so beautiful. And fit, God was that woman fit." He gave me a once-over, "You're a spitting image." I felt bile rise in my throat but I swallowed it down and poured him another glass.

"Thank you." I muttered, watching as he wobbled in his chair. He swallowed the remaining remnants from the bottle and started to pass out.

"You know, I don't know why you associate yourself with such a piece of shit. You could've had any man, but you chose him. You are just like your mother; picking the wrong guy for some easy dick. " I swallowed back the urge to to punch him in the face and quickly came to his side, helping him out of the chair, and onto his feet. "Thanks, Sweetheart." He poked my nose and helped very little in walking him back to his bedroom. I threw him on the bare mattress and started toward the door. "Where are you going?" He belched, watching me through hazed eyes.

"I'm going to clean up the kitchen and then I'll come back up so you can... Read me a bedtime story." I flashed him a smile before climbing down the steps. Finding a hammer in one of the drawers in the kitchen, I pulled the nails out of the front door that Dorian had sealed shut after my first attempt to escape. Once all the nails had been pulled out, I quietly opened the door. A cool breeze blew through the open doorway and I fluttered my eyes closed.

Freedom.

And yet suddenly I was frozen in my tracks. There was someone downstairs, I couldn't just leave them in Dorian's hands, especially after I leave. I padded over to the basement door, which creaked as I opened it and I grimaced, flicking the light on. Tiptoeing down the creaky old stairs was a painstakingly slow process, but I followed the flickering light bulbs to a dingy room where I found a body heaped on the floor. A sob racked my chest as I took in the familiar tattoos.

"Dax?" I whispered, my hand shaky as I leaned forward to touch him. He moved, his eyes squinting up at me under the bright lights. "Oh my god." Tears fell freely from my eyes, taking in the sight of Dax's body bruised and cut, his bottom lip slit open with dried blood crusted down his chin.

"Princesa, funny meeting you here," He attempted to joke, but winced as he moved, "I think my rib is broken." I craned my neck to the side to see a slight dent in his normally perfect abdomen.

"Let's get you out of here," I turned around and searched for a key, finding the brass piece of metal handing on a hook near a tool bench. I was in the middle of unlocking Dax's left cuff when a shot ripped through the silent evening air. I whipped around, finding Dorian with a pistol in his hand, pointed at Dax.

"Fuck." Dax curse and I turned my attention back to him, a bullet hole punctured his right shoulder.

"You pick him over your own father?" Dorian slurred, walking toward me. Dax pulled the key from my hands and carefully unlocked his right wrist from the cuff, slumping against the wall in pain. I stood, swallowing hard as my mental case of a biological father neared me. "He's using you for your body, Sweetheart, can't you see that? What I'm offering you is a lifetime of love that no one else can give you." I pulled out the hammer and braced myself like it were a baseball bat.

"Don't come any closer." I warned, my voice shaking.

"You wouldn't hurt your own father, would you, Sweetheart?" He cocked his head to the side and pouted. I slowly lowered the hammer and Dorian smiled, "See, everything is okay." I nodded slowly.

"It will be." I threw the hammer and Dorian dropped the gun to catch it. Quickly springing forward, I caught the firearm and pulled the trigger.

26

CHAPTER 26

Dorian's lifeless body hit the cement like a sack of potatoes. I stood like a statue for a moment, not yet registering what had happened. I killed someone. Dax's groans of pain brought me back to earth and I quickly crawled over to him, throwing the gun across the room.

"Not to be that cop, or anything, but throwing a gun is incredibly dangerous." Dax scolded, clutching his bloodied wound with his good hand.

"Give me a firearm lesson later, for now, let's focus on getting you to a hospital."

"There's no time for that, I'm bleeding too fast and too much, you need to take the bullet out." He winced, nodding toward the stairs. "Go check to see if there's a needle and thread somewhere upstairs-"

"Are you insane?" I screamed, blinking at him.

"No, I'm logical. The nearest hospital is forty minutes away, and that's just to get there. By the time we get a doctor to do what I'm asking you to do, I'll have to get the majority of my arm cut off. Now, you're studying to be a vet. Just think of me as a dog, who got shot, and you need to fix me up so I can go home to my family."

"O-Okay," I stammered, stumbling toward the stairs, "I'll be right back." I tore up the stairs and ran around the house looking for a needle. Finding nothing in the kitchen or any of the bedrooms, I finally found a mini First Aid kit in the bathroom. I clambered back down the stairs and proudly displayed the kit to Dax.

"Good, Princesa, now open it up and find what you need." Dax instructed and I did as I was told, rummaging through the kit until I found a needle and thread.

"Should I apply the alcohol towelette or-"

"No, Princesa, I need you to reach into my shoulder and pull out the bullet, okay?" He reached out with his good arm to squeeze my trembling hand. "You can do this." With a nod, I slowly moved over his wound, watching blood pulsate out of the muscle and tissue. Swallowing back my fear, I pushed my fingers through the bullet wound and felt for pieces of metal. Dax ground his teeth together in agony and I whimpered in guilt and frustration.

"I'm sorry, I'm sorry," I apologized, finally finding that the bullet had gone completely through Dax's shoulder. "The bullet is gone, there's an exit wound."

"Good, now sew them up and we'll go." He took a deep breath as I threaded the needle.

"Oh yeah, easy as pie." I mumbled, pressing the needle against his skin. "Here it goes..." I pushed it through his skin and then back through the other side. I did this over and over until the entrance wound had been sealed, and then I started on the exit. When I finished, Dax slowly stood to his feet and leaned against me for support. We climbed up the stairs and stumbled out of the front door. Red and blue lights flickered in the distance, a helicopter light shining down on us from above.

"Backup is finally here." Dax grumbled, rolling his eyes. I laughed softly, relieved that this was over. Over for good.

"Jane," Dax pulled away from me and insisted on standing on his own, "I love you and loosing you was the worst thing to ever happen to me. I need you." I smiled brightly up at him.

"I love you, too."

Dax was released from the hospital two days later and ordered to bed rest until his arm and rib fully healed. We flew back to California in a plane specifically for medical transportation, where I volunteered to take care of him until he got better. When the cab pulled up to Dax's house, I realized how long it had been since I'd been home. The grass was long and shaggy and the plants had died from lack of watering. I helped Dax settle into his bedroom, helping him undress and slip under the blankets. I kissed his forehead as the pain medication kicked in and he fell asleep. I was walking out of Dax's yard when a familiar red head popped her head out of our house.

"Jane?" She called out, running down the steps.

"Viv!" I called back, colliding into her arms. We jumped up and down, holding each other tight. I missed her; I missed her smile, her stupid yoga poses, and her girlfriend. Dalila watched us, laughing softly at our dramatic reunion and soon joined in on the hug.

"So tell me everything." Viv grinned. I laid out the entire story, including the steamy details of my first time and the news about my biological father. Dalila left an hour later to visit Dax and for just a moment, things felt like they had before I met Dax. Simple. And boring. Viv and I made a bag of pizza rolls and watched trashy reality TV. I felt like my life was falling back into place. When I finally had a moment to myself, I wandered into my bedroom where I found my phone where I had left it. My voicemail was filled with messages from Riley, asking for another chance. I scrolled through my contacts and deleted his number, placing it back on my desk.

My bed was still made the way I had left it and it felt cool against my skin as I sunk under the covers. I couldn't have been asleep long before I felt my mattress dip under some-one's weight. I drowsily flicked my lamp on and starred at the tattooed cop that had climbed into my bed.

"What are you doing here? You're supposed to be in bed." I laughed softly, shaking my head. Dax yawned and ran his fingers through his tousled hair.

"We slept together every night we were in Mexico, you can't expect me to sleep without you now." He laid on his back and pulled me across his left side, kissing my forehead. "Goodnight, Princesa."

"Goodnight, Officer Rivera." I giggled softly and pressed a kiss to the corner of his lips.

"I love you." He murmured.

"I love you, too."

27

— ◆ —

Epilogue

The bright early morning sun shown through the large bay window of the bedroom. The now familiar eggshell white walls were lit up with beams of light, causing colors of the rainbow to dance across the room. I sat up, groggy from the blissful sleep and gently moved from underneath a heavy arm. My naked body was met with cool air as the blankets slipped off of me and I pulled my satin robe across my limbs. Tying my hair up in a messy bun atop my head, I tiptoed downstairs to the kitchen where the cleanly stainless steel appliances waited to be used. Before I started, I scrolled through my phone and landed on the perfect song to make breakfast to.

"Why'all ready to get busy? (huh huh!)Now, buttermilk biscuits here we goZip the flour roll the doughClap your hands and stomp your feetMove your butt to the funky beat (huh huh)"

Within minutes, the kitchen was absorbed in lushes smells of breakfast foods as I danced around and mouthed the words to the song. In the oven were twelve buttermilk biscuits of my own creation, buttery and baking to a gold crust. On the stove, a pan of shredded potato became hash browns, sizzling gently in the cast iron. Adjacent to the pan of hash browns was another pan of sausage, browning and popping among the oil. And while everything cooked, I squeezed oranges into a pitcher to make juice.

"We from L.A. to the CarolinasDip them suckers in Aunt JemimaDon't make a difference what food you makeUse buttermilk biscuits to clean your plateYou eat 'em in the morn', you eat 'em at nightKentucky Fried Chicken makes the suckers just rightI am eat 'em with jelly it's my favorite deallyWrapped and sealed by a freak named Shelley (huh huh)"

"Why do I always find you like this?" A raspy voice called from the doorway. I spun around, horror filling my veins, caught. Dax's eyes watched me in amusement, a smirk playing on his lips. With my cheeks heated in a blush, I skipped over to him and planted a kiss on his soft lips, my fingers brushing over the bullet wound that was now a pink scar. "As much as I love to watch my girlfriend spit Sir Mix-A-Lot at seven in the morning, I wish she'd come back to bed." He leaned down, catching my lips with his once again. I giggled, squirming under this intoxicating touch.

"But I made breakfast." I pouted, my bottom lip jutting out in defiance. Dax's smirk deepened, his arms wrapping around my waist to lift me and set me on the counter of the island.

"How sweet is my Princesa?" He cooed, his hand pressing my chest down to lay me on my back, "How can I ever repay her?"

Dax's large hands grazed up my thigh and I sucked in a deep breath, my legs beginning to shake. Moving to the stove, Dax flicked off the burners and repositioned himself between my legs. His hands flirted with my pelvic bone, tracing soft circles into the skin. I hummed in satisfaction, looking down at him as he teased me.

-Mature Content below-

"What about breakfast?" I whispered breathily, biting my bottom lip between my teeth. Dax nodded in agreement.

"You're absolutely right." He drifted over to the cupboard and pulled out maple syrup. Dax flicked the top off and made his way back over to me, pressing the bottle's spout against my cl!t. "Now it's breakfast." I gasped at the sensation of the thick syrup dripping down my sex. Dax groaned at the sight, licking his lips in anticipation. Setting the bottle down beside me, Dax wasted no time, his tongue lapping up the sweet sap from between my folds. Taking my cl!t into his mouth, his teeth gently grazed the bundle of nerves before his tongue swirled around it in figure-eights. I arched my back and used the edge of the island to brace myself, the edges of my vision clouding in pleasure.

"Dax," I moaned out while his tongue assaulted my womanhood. Dax sucked two fingers into his mouth, his eyes staring into mine as he did so.

"Tell me what you want, Nena." He growled softly, his wet fingers rubbing vicious circles against my cl!t.

"Your fingers, please, your fingers." I begged, knowing it turned Dax on. "Please, Papi." At the sound of the his pet name, Dax's eyes clouded over with lust and he plunged his fingers into my sex, giving me no time to adjust before pumping them in and out of me. I cried out, unable to control the profanities that left my lips.

"Do you like that, Princesa? My fingers buried in that sweet little pnssy?" He glowered down at me in need, taking in the sight of my vulnerability.

"Yes, Papi, yes!" I cried out, my eyes fluttering as I neared my orgasm.

"Do you want my c!ck, Nena?" He whispered to me soothingly, offering me a release. I nodded eagerly and Dax carried me from the island to the dining room table, standing me at the foot of it and bending me over. My stomach laid across the table, my ass fully displayed to Dax as he slid his tip through my folds. "Beg for me, Princesa." He growled, twisting his knuckles around my hair and pulling my head backward, my back arching with the movement.

"Fuck me, Papi, please fuck me." I whimpered, my feet standing on their tiptoes. Dax, not usually so quick to end my begging, plunged into me with need of his own, fucking into me relentlessly. I recoiled against his thrusts, my body bouncing with each hard drive into me. His hard member splitting me open with its size, something I never seemed to get used to despite the countless amount of times we had slept together.

Dax lifted my left leg onto the table, leaving me standing with one leg as he drilled into me from a new angle. My mouth fell open, my eyes fluttering to the back of my head. "Please don't stop," I begged again, enjoying the sheer dominance radiating from his body.

"I'll never stop, Princesa, not until you come undone around me. I want to feel your walls tighten around my c!ck, I want to hear you scream my name so everyone knows you're my girl." He ground his hips into mine, "Who's girl are you?"

"Yours," I mouthed, my knuckles turning white against the wooden table.

"That's right, Nena, now tell me who's man I am?" He leaned down to graze his lips across mine, his hips still bucking against mine.

"Mine." I grinned, our eyes transfixed on one another until I did exactly as Dax had described. I came, my walls tightening around his member, milking his own release. I screamed his name, my throat feeling sore for overuse. Dax nuzzled the crook of my neck, peppering its base with kisses. I giggled from beneath him and he carried me back into the kitchen.

-Mature Scene Over-

With my robe retied around me, Dax plated the breakfast I had prepared for the two of us and we dug in. Dax moaned softly as he bit into a warm biscuit, satisfaction drawn on his face. I smiled and we finished breakfast. Dax hopped into the shower to get ready for work while I stayed home like the lazy bum that I was. Because of my absence while I was in Mexico, I was fired from the bakery and despite Dax's threat to 'sue the sons of bitches who fired his girl,' I was still out of work. My phone chirped at my side and I slid my finger across the screen, accepting the call.

"Hey, Viv, what's up?" I greeted into the phone, organizing my backpack for tomorrow's day at school.

"Nothing, Dalila and I were working out in our home gym," She sighed into the phone before continuing, "You may remember it was your old room before you moved in with Dax." I rolled my eyes.

"Yes, I remember." I chuckled, slipping my planner into my backpack.

"Then you will also remember that from the window, we can see directly into Dax's house." I paled, swallowing dryly.

"What did you see?" I questioned in a low voice, my heart in my ears.

"Oh nothing, just Dax's face buried in your snatch." She replied, her volume increasing with each word, "Do you people own drapes?"

"I'll look into it." I laughed softly, my cheeks stinging with embarrassment as I hung up. Dax exited from the shower, small beads of water cascading down his muscled body while a plush white towel wrapped loosely around his hips. I glanced at the clock. Damn. No time for round two. I watched Dax as he moved around the room, pulling on his uniform piece by piece, his badge, his gun in its holster.

"What?" He chuckled, noticing my stare. I shook my head.

"Nothing, I'm just happy." Dax strode across the room and pressed a soft kiss to my forehead. I walked him to the front door where he slipped on his shoes and pulled me into a passionate kiss.

"I love you, Princesa." He pressed one last kiss to my temple before opening the door and skipping down the steps. I leaned in the doorway of our home, watching him pull out of the driveway.

"I love you, too, Officer Rivera."